D1282775

PABLOS
and the BULL

*To my friends, the Librarians in the
Bonnyrigg District Library,
Midlothian County Libraries,
who gave me so much help in my
research for the background to
this book*

PABLOS
and the BULL

Kathleen Fidler

Blackie

ISBN 0 216 90822 1

Blackie and Son Limited
Bishopbriggs
Glasgow G64 2NZ
Furnival House, 14–18 High Holborn
London WC1V 6BX

Printed in Great Britain by
The Anchor Press Ltd, Tiptree, Essex

Contents

1 Attack by Pirates

Pablos, the herd-boy, sat on the grass just below the rocky outcrop that overlooked his village. The sun was warm and Pablos was contented. A small black bull calf lay beside him, contented too, for his stomach was full of young tender grass. Pablos munched at his dinner of coarse barley-bread and goat's cheese and a handful of wild grapes he had plucked on his way to the upland pasture. Every now and again he held out a piece of bread and cheese and Niro, the bull calf, took it gently from his hand.

There was a great understanding between Pablos and Niro because Pablos had fed and cared for the bull from the time when Niro's mother had died—an hour after his birth. It was then that Pablos had made a feeding bag from a sheep's bladder and filled it with milk from other cows and persuaded Niro to suck at it. Almost by a miracle Niro survived, and from that time the bull followed Pablos as if he were his mother.

Pablos lived at a farm not far from the village of Corinth, a slave-boy to his Greek master. He was taller than most Greek boys of his age and was not dark of skin like them, but fair-haired and blue-eyed. His mother was a slave too, taken in a raid on a far northern shore where fair-haired people dwelled and she had been sold with her young son to their master in Corinth. Pablos had grown up as a valued slave on his master's farm, for he was clever with animals, especially the cows and bulls. Now he was twelve years old and his master had shown his approval by entrusting the young bull to him. As slave masters went, he was a good one, not beating Pablos too hard or too often and feeding him sufficiently. All the same, when Pablos listened to his mother's tales of the north country he longed to be free, free to roam the seas, free to make a life for himself, to belong only to himself and to no other person.

As the boy lay on the grass, raised on his elbows with his chin cupped in his hands, he looked towards the sea and dreamed his dreams of freedom while Niro softly chewed the cud beside him. All around him flowers blazed in the pasture: golden ox-eyed daisies, blue cornflowers and purple vetches. Below him in another pasture the cows were grazing and below that were the scattered fishermen's cottages bordering the Saronic Gulf with its many islands. Away over the hill was the larger village of Corinth that looked out on to another sea. Pablos wondered idly what places and people lay beyond the two seas, one to the east and the other to the west. Perhaps someday he would find out.

All at once his eye caught the movement of two ships in the Gulf to the east. They had appeared from behind a small headland and seemed to be creeping stealthily along the shore. There was no doubt that they were making for the small sheltered harbour that served the fishermen of the village. Pablos stiffened. Of course they might be peaceful traders bringing goods from foreign lands, but the trading ships usually went to Corinth. There had been talk among the village folk gathered round their fires at night of pirates along the coasts of Hellas and Akhaia.

Pablos watched the boats as they beat up the Gulf. He wondered whether to go down to the village and warn the folk of the approaching ships, but if they were just peaceful traders he would be laughed at for his pains and perhaps even get a beating for bringing down his bull from the pasture before nightfall. Pablos decided to stay where he was and watch. Perhaps the ships were making for some other harbour.

He had not long to wait. Suddenly the ships turned towards the village. Under a south-easterly breeze they moved quickly. In a few minutes they had reached the rough stone mole that sheltered the harbour. There the sailors leaped ashore and tied their ships to the big stones that served the fishermen as bollards. Pablos could see the ships more clearly now. They were long ships, much longer than the fishermen's caiques—almost a hundred feet long, with a central mast and big square sail, and a row of fifteen oars on each side. They rode the water high at the prow and the sterns were high too, with a raised gangway between the prow and the small rear deck. At the prow was a ram, a wicked-looking bronze spike to pierce the sides of other ships. At the stern was a large 'sweep' or steering oar. Pablos could now see that these were not peaceful merchantmen. He rose to his feet and shaded his eyes with his hands the better to watch them.

From the body of the ship a number of men ran along the gangplank and leaped ashore. The sun glinted on the wicked two-headed axes that they carried. They rushed towards the fishermen's huts. At this time of the day most of the men were away fishing or working in the fields. The huts would only be occupied by a few of the women. Pablos watched, horrified. From the village rose shouts and screams as the women poured out of their houses and tried to make for the woods. They did not get far before their attackers were upon them. But the pirates' real purpose was to plunder and to steal cattle and so most of them left their pursuit of the women and returned to ransack the houses, carrying off household goods and woollen garments.

As Pablos watched, there was a puff of smoke, then a sudden blaze from the roof of one of the houses, followed by another and another. The raiders were firing the thatched roofs, tinder-dry in the hot sun. Only a touch from a torch was needed.

Pablos clenched his fists. "If only I were a grown man with an axe . . ." he muttered.

Suddenly one of the raiders shouted and pointed up the hill. At first it seemed to Pablos that the man was pointing directly at him. Then he realised that he was pointing at the herd of cows half-way down the hill below him. The raiders rushed towards the hill.

"Perhaps they'll stop at the cows and come no further up the hill," Pablos said to himself. "They mustn't find Niro. We must hide."

Behind him was a low outcrop of rock with a narrow hollow between it and the rising cliffs behind. Pablos seized the plaited rush-rope that tethered Niro.

"Come, Niro! After me!" he hissed.

Niro had learned to obey him as a tiny calf and quietly followed him behind the rocks which screened them from the men below.

Pablos sank to his knees. "Down!" he commanded and the young bull stretched out on the earth beside him. "Quiet, now!" Pablos ordered. He found a niche between the rocks from which he could watch what went on in the meadow below. The raiders had just reached the seven cows in the pasture.

"Drive the cows down to the shore. We'll kill them there," the leader shouted to his men.

In the clear air his words reached Pablos. To his astonishment the man spoke in Greek though with an outlandish accent. "Achaeans?" he muttered. "Raiders!"

Pablos watched the cows being rounded up and cruelly beaten with sticks. One cow bellowed in pain and anger. This was too much for Niro. Those cows were his family. He raised his head above the rocky screen and bellowed angrily in return.

"Down, Niro, down!" Pablos cried desperately but he was too late. The leader of the raiders turned from beating the cow and looked up the hill just in time to see Niro's long horns disappearing behind the rocks.

"There's a bull up there!" he yelled to his men. "I'm going to look for it. Come with me, Hippias! The rest of you drive the cows down to the sea."

Pablos's heart turned to stone. He had no hope of escaping with Niro to the mountain above. The raiders would move more quickly than he and Niro. There was no hope of reaching his master's farm over the hill, and he could not bear to see Niro driven down to the shore and a knife thrust into his throat. He rose to his feet and Niro with him and faced the two men as they rushed up the hill towards him.

"Aye, it's a young bull right enough, Kylon," Hippias called. "There'll be good steaks for eating beside the fire tonight."

Pablos's blood ran cold. He felt sick at the thought of Niro being butchered and eaten. Maybe the men would kill him first? If he had to die it would be better to put on a bold front and try to save Niro. He faced the men bravely.

"If you kill the bull it will bring you bad fortune," he shouted. "This bull is sacred to the god Zeus. Zeus will punish you."

The men halted, astonished. "What young cub have we

II

here?" Hippias exclaimed. "We'll deal with him first. *He's* not sacred to Zeus!" He seized Pablos by the arm and made as if to strike him with the club.

"Come to me, Niro!" Pablos yelled. Niro let out an angry bellow and moved towards the men, lowering his horns and stamping his feet.

"If you kill me the bull will kill you!" Pablos cried.

The man hesitated, his club upraised, and looked at the angry bull. He let his arm fall to his side.

"Stop, Niro!" Pablos called. "Stand still!"

The bull raised his horns and looked towards Pablos.

"Wait, Hippias! Do not strike!" said the older man. "Here is something which needs questioning. Does the bull obey you, lad?" he asked Pablos.

"You have seen it for yourself," Pablos told him boldly.

"What else can you order him to do?"

Pablos held out a hand towards Niro. "Come!" he said simply. Niro turned towards him obediently. "Kneel!" Pablos commanded. This was the latest trick he had taught Niro. He prayed that Niro would remember it. There was a moment's hesitation.

"Kneel! Kneel, Niro!" Pablos ordered desperately, pointing to the ground. Then Niro went down on his front knees!

"Is the boy a son of the god that the bull obeys him?" Hippias exclaimed.

"It might well be," Kylon said. "Perhaps we should not kill him either, for fear of the vengeance of Zeus."

Pablos was quick to see the advantage he had gained.

"If you killed the bull what advantage would that be to you after you had eaten his flesh? He could be worth more to you alive than dead. He is a fine bull who might be a breeder of other fine bulls when he is grown."

"The lad is right," Kylon said. "A bull who obeys commands like that would fetch a good price. We might sell him at Knossos."

"You would first have to get him on your ship," Pablos said boldly. "He would not obey *your* commands, only mine."

"Will he follow you?" Kylon asked.

"If I tell him to."

Kylon laughed. "It seems then that we shall have to take you to Knossos too."

Pablos saw a sudden ray of hope both for himself and Niro.

"If you promise not to slay the bull I'll lead him on to the ship for you, but you must let me come aboard with him."

Hippias frowned. "He is an impudent lad."

"I like a lad with courage. We might sell him well too, for a slave."

"How do you know that he won't lead us into a trap?" Hippias asked.

"If the bull won't follow him we shall soon know, and you can stick your dagger into his ribs then, Hippias," Kylon said. "We are wasting time. If we don't get aboard soon the men from Corinth will have armed themselves and come over the hill. We must get away. Order your bull to follow you, boy!"

At least he had gained some time, Pablos thought. From then on he would meet each danger and problem as it came up. At least he and Niro would be together on the pirates' ship.

"Come, Niro! Follow me!" he said and took hold of the rope about the bull's neck. Niro at once fell in behind Pablos and trotted obediently in his wake. They went down the hill towards the waiting boat.

The shore was a scene of slaughter and blood. The other raiders had slain the cows and skinned them for the leather hides and now they were cutting up the flesh for meat. Pablos shuddered when he thought of what might have been Niro's fate. Niro, too, bellowed at the sight and smell of the blood and pawed the ground. Pablos was afraid he might go mad. Kylon saw the danger too.

"Better get the bull aboard the ship at once," he said to Hippias.

"Shall I put an end to the boy first then?" Hippias said, feeling for his dagger.

"No. We might need him to calm the bull on the ship. Besides, we can sell him with the bull if he shows his tricks in the Market Place at Knossos. The two together might fetch a good price. Get the bull aboard!" he ordered Pablos abruptly.

There was a broad plank leading from the shore to the ship. At the foot of it Pablos stopped. "Up! Go on!" he said to Niro but the bull set his forefeet firmly in the sand and refused to budge.

"What did I tell you?" Hippias began, but Pablos cried, "This is something I have not yet taught him, to go aboard a ship. He is afraid of the water beneath the plank, but if I go first, I think he will follow me."

"If he doesn't, your days are ended," Hippias told him with a curl of his lip.

Pablos knew his life depended on Niro's obedience. He could only rely on the deep bond between him and the bull. Niro loved and trusted him. He took a deep breath, put a foot on the plank, gave a tug to the halter and said, "Come, Niro! Follow me!"

Niro gave an uneasy bellow and it seemed at first as if he would draw back.

"Come *on*!" Pablos cried desperately and took another couple of steps on the plank. Niro gave a frightened look about him but the sight of two fierce men at his rear, one with a dagger and the other with a club, persuaded him that he must follow Pablos. He stepped on to the plank, his feet clattering and slipping a little.

"Come on, Niro!" Pablos gave an impatient tug at the halter. The bull came after him. Another few steps and he was on the ship.

"Where shall I take him now?" Pablos called over his shoulder to Kylon.

Kylon pointed to the stern where a small deck made a roof for the space below. "Take your bull under there. You will find a ring to which you can tether him."

Niro was frightened at the swaying of the ship on the waves and seemed at first unwilling to step down into the little hold. Pablos felt in his leather bag and drew out a piece of barley-bread and cheese and held it out temptingly to the bull. Then he backed down into the open hold. Niro had always shared Pablos's meals and the sight of the familiar snack renewed the love and trust he had for the boy. He stepped after him into the hold. Pablos gave him the bread and said, "Lie down!" and he himself sat down beside Niro.

From the darkness of the hold came a frightened whimper. Pablos leaned forward and put out a hand. "Who is there?" Another frightened cry answered him. His hand touched an arm and he gave a tug at it. A young girl crawled towards him. She pointed to the bull, gibbering with fear.

"He won't hurt you," Pablos told her reassuringly. "He's a gentle bull. See! He likes me to stroke him."

The girl looked a little less frightened.

"Who are you? How did you get here?" Pablos asked.

"The men took me." She pointed to the shore where the raiders were carrying the hides and cow-meat to the ships.

"In a raid?" Pablos asked.

"Yes. My parents were killed but the big pirate said they could sell me for a slave to a court lady at Knossos."

Pablos guessed from her speech that she was from Akhaia.

"Where was your home?" he asked.

"Patras, where the sea widens to the west."

"Sit down beside me. The bull won't harm you," Pablos told her.

She came nearer but kept Pablos between herself and the bull. Hungrily she eyed the bread and cheese that Pablos still held in his hand but she said nothing. She had large dark eyes that looked at him beseechingly.

"Are you hungry?" Pablos asked her suddenly.

She nodded but she did not beg from him. Pablos divided the bread and cheese into three parts, one for himself and one for Niro, and the third portion he held out to the girl.

She hesitated. "For me?"

"Yes."

"I . . . I haven't eaten for two days. They gave me a little water but no food."

"Then eat now," Pablos told her. "We are both captives."

"They took you too?"

Pablos nodded.

"And the bull?"

His brow grew dark. "They only spared me because of the bull. I've taught the bull to obey some commands.

They're planning to sell us together in some place called Knossos."

"That's what I heard them say they would do with me." She shivered unhappily. "I shall be a *slave*."

"I have nearly always been a slave. It's not too bad if you get a good master," Pablos tried to reassure her but the girl looked miserable at the thought. "All the same, I've always wanted to be free to live my own life, to see other places. Have you heard the raiders say where they mean to go?"

"I overheard them talking last night. They mentioned an island called Thera and an island beyond that but I didn't catch the name."

Pablos nodded. "I've heard of Thera. Well, we'll just have to see what happens. Maybe we'll get a chance to escape."

"Escape!"

"Ssh!" Pablos put a finger to his mouth. "They mustn't hear us talking about it. We must seem to be quiet and afraid. What is your name?"

"Zirza."

"I've never heard that name before."

"My people came from far away beyond the mountains many years ago, before even my father and mother were born but they still kept the old names. They were a wandering people."

Pablos nodded. He had heard of the tribes beyond the great mountains to the north who followed their flocks of sheep from place to place and dwelled in leather tents. They were darker-skinned than the Greek people and their eyes were large and beautiful as the girl's were.

"What's your name?" she asked in her turn.

Pablos, and my bull is Niro." Pablos gave Niro a gentle pat.

"He is very quiet, not like the wild bulls my grandfather told me about."

"I've looked after him since he was born," Pablos explained. "He'll grow up to be a fine bull. I never want to be parted from him."

On shore the raiders had finished skinning the hides from the cows and cutting up the meat. Some of the crew had been roasting the meat over fires. Now they came back to the two ships and loaded hides and meat aboard near the high prows. The rowers took their places, thirty of them to each ship, fifteen on each side with a yard or two between them.

"Push off from the land!" Kylon told his crew. "There's an uninhabited island an hour's sailing away. There we'll put in for the night and eat."

The leading rower pushed his long sweeping oar into the water. Each man behind him watched for his signal and when he dipped his oar in the water they followed suit. The thirty oars dipped and rose, dipped and rose, in a strong, steady rhythm. When they were well out from the coast four men amidships hoisted a single brown sail. The wind and the tide bore them away. Behind them they left the burnt homes and the blood on the foreshore.

2 The Wreck

The two children cowered under the decking at the stern, and Pablos noticed that the freshening breeze was making Zirza shiver.

"Are you cold?" he asked. "Lie down beside the bull. He'll keep you warm."

Zirza hesitated. She was still afraid of the bull.

"Niro won't hurt you," Pablos assured her. "He's very gentle. He's used to me sleeping close to him." He made a space between himself and the bull and Zirza, still fearful, crept into it. Niro stirred a little and opened one eye sleepily, but at Pablos's command, "Quiet, Niro!" he settled down to sleep again.

For an hour nothing was heard save the creak of the sail against the mast, the grunts of the rowers as they bent to their work and the slap of the waves against the ship's timbers. The day grew into twilight, a short twilight which would soon sink into night. A dark shape loomed against the fading sunset sky.

Kylon pointed. "There is the island. Turn the ship towards it."

The man at the stern pulled the long steering oar over to the right and the galley began to come round towards the land. They reached a small bay with headlands like horns protecting it on either side. The rowers brought the ship close inshore. The single sail was brought down and furled and a boulder with a leather rope attached was thrown overboard to anchor the ship.

Kylon handed out chunks of meat and bread to the rowers who wolfed it down. Almost as an after-thought he threw some to Pablos and Zirza under the decking. The meat was almost raw and Zirza looked at it with disgust remembering the cruel slaughter of the cows.

"Try to eat some of it," Pablos coaxed. "It may be a long time before they give us anything else to eat." He dropped his voice. "You may need all your strength later if we try to escape. I'll share my bread with Niro."

Zirza did her best to obey his advice and choked down a few mouthfuls of meat and bread.

When the rowers had eaten some of them fell asleep at once over their oars but others waded ashore and found more comfortable places for themselves on a grassy slope just above the beach. The moon rose and shone brilliantly over the island. Pablos put his head outside the covered hold. Kylon saw him and strode over the planking to look inside.

"Well, lad, what is it? Is the bull all right?"

"Yes, but he's hungry too," Pablos said. "What am I to feed him on? Have you any grain?"

"Grain? Why would my ship carry grain? I'm not a miserable trader."

"If you want to get a good price for the bull he must be in good condition. With no food he'll soon become thin," Pablos told Kylon boldly.

"That lad should have his tongue cut out for his impudence," Hippias muttered, fingering the long bronze knife at his belt.

"No. He speaks sense. But how is the bull to be fed?"

Pablos spoke up again. "There's grass beyond the shore. If you let us take him to it he can eat his fill and that will last him for a day at least."

"Ha! It is just a plot of the boy's to run away," Hippias snorted.

"How could I get away from the island without a boat?" Pablos asked.

"There are no people on the island so where could he go?" Kylon pointed out. "If the bull is tied to a stake, it cannot get away either but it could eat in a circle round the stake." Kylon lowered his voice and spoke to Hippias. "I don't think the lad would try to get away without his bull. He sets such store by it." He turned to Pablos again. "You will give me your word to bring the bull back on board?"

"I promise you that," Pablos replied. "Will you let the girl come too? We are both stiff from lying in the hold and she'll help me to herd the bull back again."

"Are you going to give her the chance to run away too?" Hippias sneered.

"Where could either of them go?" Kylon asked. "There's no food or shelter for them here. We risk nothing by letting them go ashore with the bull. *They* can't live on grass. We want them to be able to move about easily when we offer them for sale as slaves, and their limbs have been cramped in that narrow space. Another couple of days and we'll have them off our hands and sold."

Pablos pricked up his ears. Another couple of days? That must mean a short voyage. Would that be to the coast of Greece or to one of the large islands? He must be ready for any chance of escape, but he was determined to take Niro with him. And now there was the girl to think of, too. It was going to be difficult. Meanwhile he had the problem of getting Niro ashore and back on the ship again.

"Up, Niro!" he ordered and obediently the little bull

rose on his knees and then to his feet. Zirza rose too, staggering a little, for her legs were stiff.

Pablos urged Niro down the plank. When the bull saw the fresh green grass beyond the sandy shore, he needed little prodding. He stepped cautiously down the gang-plank with Pablos's hand on the back of his neck, but once he set foot on the ground, he gave a joyful bellow and set off at a quick trot. Pablos held on to his plaited rush-rope and was tugged along too, while Zirza tried to keep up with them. Kylon and Hippias followed hard on their heels.

As soon as they reached the grass Niro's head went down and he began to feed. Hippias took the rope from Pablos and hitched it round a tree trunk. "The bull will have plenty of room to graze in a circle. We'll be keeping a close watch on you," he said, a hint of a threat in his voice.

"No need to trouble. The lad won't stray far from his bull," Kylon told him. The two men returned to the ship.

Pablos sat down on the grass near Niro. Zirza stayed beside him but she did not sit down. She looked towards the belt of trees and bushes which surrounded the grassy slope. In the bright moonlight the bushes were plain to be seen.

"The men won't think it strange if you go behind those bushes," Pablos said in a low voice to Zirza. "Among them are some mulberries and wild grapes. I've put my leather wallet on the ground behind Niro. Pick it up as you go and fill it as full as you can with berries and grapes. But first look for a stone and lay it at the bottom of the wallet. It must be a sharp, flat stone with an edge like a knife. Put the berries on top to hide it."

Zirza looked at him questioningly.

"We have no weapons. A sharp stone might be useful," Pablos said.

Zirza nodded. She waited till Pablos went to speak to Niro and then she quickly picked up the leather bag and went towards the bushes. When she returned Pablos was again sitting near the bull. She dropped the bag beside him.

"Well?" Pablos said.

"I did as you said." She handed Pablos a bunch of wild grapes. "The stone is at the bottom of the bag."

"Well done!"

When they had eaten the grapes they settled down to sleep on the grass as the rest of the crew were doing, while Niro munched contentedly at the end of his rope.

As soon as the sun rose there was a bustle to get aboard. With Hippias watching him closely Pablos unhitched Niro from the tree and urged him back to the ship. Niro was unwilling to leave his patch of green grass and bellowed indignantly.

"You should take a stick to that bull," Hippias said impatiently.

"I've never used a stick on him in all his life," Pablos declared hotly.

"Then it's time someone used a stick on both of you." Hippias cut a switch from one of the bushes but by that time the bull was following Pablos up the gangplank and into the ship.

"No matter! The switch will serve for another time," Hippias muttered.

Pablos heard him. "If he so much as touches my bull with that switch he'll pay for it," he declared under his breath. He clutched the leather bag under his arm. Kylon noticed him.

"What have you got in there?" he asked.

At once Pablos opened the leather bag. "Mulberries and grapes. The girl picked them. They're for her. She doesn't like the meat."

Kylon broke off a small bunch of grapes and crammed them into his mouth but he did not delve further into the bag.

"Get the bull under the deck quickly," he said. He himself tied the bull to the ring in the bulwarks.

"Lie down, Niro." Pablos prodded the bull. Zirza was there already, but no longer crouching in a corner as she had done the previous day. She had overcome her fear of the bull. She patted him on the shoulder as he got down. The bull looked at her with gentle eyes.

The rowers returned at Kylon's sharp command.

"Get moving! We have a long voyage before us. I want to make the island of Crete by nightfall."

"Crete!" Pablos whispered to Zirza. "Crete? Is that where they want to sell my bull?"

Zirza nodded. "I've heard that they use bulls for their entertainment in Crete. There's a sport where boys—and girls too—have to catch the bull by the horns and leap over his back." She shuddered slightly. "If the acrobats aren't quick enough, they can be gored to death by the bull. That amuses the crowds!"

Pablos asked, "How do you know all this?"

"Boys and girls have been carried off by pirates and sold. Perhaps that's why they didn't kill me. Once, the men of my tribe captured a pirate from Crete and he told them about this cruel sport. That's why I am frightened of bulls—except this one."

"You—you think they might use you as a bull-leaper?" Pablos looked shocked.

"I'll be sold as a slave and whoever buys me can do what he wants with me. The Cretan told us that the nobles of the King's court put their slaves into the Bull Sports and then lay bets on how long they will last before they're killed." Zirza shuddered again.

"Then we must do our best to escape."

"How can we escape? Into the sea?" Zirza sounded despairing.

"If we have to. Can you swim?"

"Yes."

"Swim well?"

"Well enough."

"Then maybe we'll have a chance when we're near the land. That's why I wanted the sharp stone."

"But if you try to kill one of these men the rest will kill you."

"I don't mean to kill anyone. Against thirty men I wouldn't have a chance. No, I wanted the sharp stone to cut Niro's tether quickly."

"You think we can escape *with* the bull?" Zirza sounded surprised.

"I wouldn't go without him," Pablos said staunchly.

Zirza shook her head doubtfully. "That makes escape sound impossible."

"We'll see. Don't speak so loudly. Kylon and Hippias mustn't hear us."

The rowers had now settled down to a steady rhythm. The sail was hoisted and the ship moved eastward towards the rising sun. Against the primrose sky many islands were silhouetted, but the ship drew away from the islands, keeping well out from their shores. Then, as the sun rose higher the steersman gave a sharp turn to his steering oar at the stern and the ship turned in a great curve to the south. A northerly breeze held the sail taut and flecked the crests of the waves with white spume as it speeded the ship along.

"The wind's freshening," Hippias said to Kylon.

"Yes, we're running well before it. At this speed we should make Crete by nightfall."

The wind grew stronger and the seas rougher. The sky to the north and west became dark and overcast.

"There's a storm brewing." Kylon looked uneasily westward. He knew the sudden Mediterranean storms only too well. "Let's hope we make port before it breaks. It'll be dark early and we don't want to spend the night tossing among the rocks."

The ship ran on before the rising storm, lifting to the crests and pitching into the troughs between the waves. Conditions aboard the ship grew more and more uncomfortable and spray drenched the rowers as they toiled at their oars. Water began to collect in the small hold under the stern deck and Pablos and Zirza shivered as they sat in it. Zirza was sea-sick. Pablos moved a little nearer the entrance lest he should be sea-sick too. Even Niro shifted about unhappily and Pablos put a restraining hand on him to stop him from flinging his weight to one side and crushing Zirza. Once the bull bellowed in fear.

"Keep that beast still and quiet or we'll fling him overboard and you with him!" Hippias threatened.

"Quiet, Niro. Lie down," Pablos commanded.

"What's going to happen to us?" Zirza asked in a trembling voice.

"Nothing. Keep still and wait," Pablos told her in a low whisper.

An inch or two at a time, he moved towards the ring to which Niro was tethered, keeping an eye on Hippias all the time. His hand searched the depths of his leather knapsack for the sharp stone. A rower seemed to be flagging and Hippias went to whip him on with cruel blows. Quick as lightning Pablos had the sharp stone out and he cut through the plaited rushes of Niro's tether, pulling the rope towards him and concealing the cut ends within his hand.

"At least you are free, Niro," he muttered. "You will stand a chance of swimming if he does fling you overboard."

The storm grew worse and the skies darker. Night began to fall. Over in the east a fire shone on the horizon and made the pall of cloud above it a rosy pink. Kylon was standing near them, holding on to the side of the open hold to steady himself. Pablos was so astonished at the sight of the fire that he exclaimed and pointed. "What is that over there?"

Kylon laughed at the boy's surprise. "That? That's the burning mountain of the island of Thera. I've heard it called a volcano. It growls like a mountain bear sometimes. It's not always as bright as it is tonight. Sometimes the fire in the heart of the mountain sinks so it can't be seen at all. I'm glad to see it tonight, though, for it's like a beacon pointing the way to Crete."

Pablos looked at the isle of Thera with foreboding. There was something sinister in that cloud of fire. Soon they left the island far behind them, with its high cliffs and fiery crown.

The storm grew worse. Great rolling seas swept the galley along. Suddenly there was a terrific crack and the sail was whipped away by the wind. Now the galley had to depend on the rowers, whose oars sometimes dipped deep into the water and sometimes flailed uselessly in the air. It was impossible for the rowers to keep time with each other's strokes, no matter how Hippias stood over them with his whip and shouted and threatened. Some men collapsed unconscious over their oars. The wind seemed to come at them from all directions, making huge hollows and mountains of the waves as the galley went twisting and corkscrewing among them.

"Oh, Pablos! What is going to happen to us?" Zirza gasped.

Pablos was frightened himself, but he tried to keep calm.

"Listen, Zirza! Put your hands beside mine on Niro's rope. Whatever happens, hang on to it and don't let go! Even if we're flung into the sea!"

Zirza gripped the rush-rope. The ship ploughed on through the mountainous seas. Then, to the south, the long dark outline of a rocky shore appeared.

"Crete!" Kylon shouted to Hippias, pointing south, but there was no relief in his voice. The high cliffs and jagged rocks looked too grim and menacing as the waves hurled them towards it. Though the steersman tried to keep the ship's prow heading into the waves, it was in vain. Soon he had lost all control of the ship's direction and the waves drove it along as if it were a cork on the water. Nearer and nearer came the dark shore. Then, suddenly, the galley was twisted broadside in the trough of a wave. A huge crest hung above the ship for a moment, then crashed down upon it. In a minute the galley filled with water and the rowers were flung struggling into the furious sea. The stern of the ship did not sink immediately. The air imprisoned under the deck seemed to hold it up and in that minute's space Pablos pushed Niro from under the deck. Half blinded by the water Zirza held on to Niro's rope, Pablos beside her. Gasping, swallowing the sea-water, she still held on as she had been told to do. The stern began to sink under them, then another wave flung them clear of the sinking ship, but Pablos and Zirza still held on to Niro's halter. The next wave carried them clear of the wreckage and Pablos, Zirza and the bull were still together in the boiling sea. As they were lifted to the crest of a wave Pablos saw the outline of rocks and cliffs immediately ahead. He gave Niro a push towards them.

"Swim, Niro, swim!" he cried. These were not commands that the bull understood, but his natural instincts forced him to strike out with his four sturdy little legs. Zirza was still hanging on to his rope and Pablos was clutching the end of it.

"If you can swim, then use your legs too!" Pablos yelled at Zirza, as he kicked away in a swimming stroke.

Both children had been brought up on the shores of a warm sea and had spent their childhood in and out of the water, almost as much at home in it as on land. Being able to swim helped them now, even among these huge and terrifying waves. Towed by Niro they kicked out and took the strain off his rope. The little bull struggled valiantly towards the land. Sometimes the waves seemed to bring them nearer: sometimes the undertow seemed to drag them back again.

Zirza's kicks became feebler. Pablos edged along the rope towards her and helped to support her with one arm. Still Niro struggled on. Then, all at once, Pablos felt his feet touch something. Again a wave lifted them, then once again Pablos felt the beach beneath him. So did Niro and he began struggling and panting up a steep bank of sand, pulling the children after him as they still clutched the rope. The water sank from Pablos's shoulder to his knees. Half dragging, half supporting Zirza he fought his way to the top of the sand bank, through dwindling shallows and at last on to dry sand. Niro, winded now, sank to his knees and Pablos with him. Zirza had lost consciousness. Pablos rolled her over on to her face and opened her mouth so she could bring up the sea-water she had swallowed. He slapped and rubbed her back hard. At last she gurgled and vomited up the sea-water. When the fit of sickness had passed she opened her eyes and stared about her.

"Where are we?" she gasped.

"On an island beach somewhere." All at once Pablos felt exhausted. "We must lie here till we get our strength back."

He lay on the sand, first stretching out a hand to Niro lying beside him. The little bull gave his hand a warm lick then weariness overcame them all and they slept, huddled into a protecting hollow in the sand. Above them the wind shrieked among the stars as it rolled back the heavy clouds.

3 The Slaves of Khani

When Pablos awoke the wind had died down and the sun was already high in the south-east. He gazed about him. They were lying on the sands of a shallow bay between two headlands where the hills came down to the sea. The bull was awake too and stirring uneasily. Zirza was lying very still, so still that Pablos felt a stab of fear in his heart. He crawled over the sand to her and felt her hand. It was cold but not with the cold of death. A pulse still beat in her wrist. To reassure himself Pablos held a flat cold pebble to her mouth. To his relief the pebble misted over with her breath. Zirza was alive. Pablos gave a thankful sigh.

Niro rose and stamped impatiently with his little hoofs as he stared about him.

"What are you looking for? Grass?" Pablos asked. "I'm hungry and thirsty too." Thirsty? His tongue felt swollen and his mouth parched and dry. He shook Zirza. "Wake up, Zirza! We must find fresh water as soon as we can before the sun gets any higher."

Zirza opened her eyes slowly. She looked surprised to find herself lying on a sandy beach.

"How did we get here?"

"By the mercy of the gods and with the help of Niro. But now he's thirsty and hungry and so am I. We must find water to drink and pasture for him. Can you get up, Zirza?"

Zirza felt stiff and all her limbs ached but she struggled to her feet. "Where shall we look for water?" she began

31

to ask but Niro answered that question for her. He suddenly set off at a gallop towards the circle of cliffs round the bay. Pablos raced after him and grabbed at the rush-rope that still dangled from his neck.

"Come on, Zirza!" he yelled. "The bull will lead us to water and to grass." Zirza followed them at a slower pace. She still felt dizzy with exhaustion.

Pablos was right. When Zirza caught up with them Niro had found a small stream that ran down to the beach. Already the bull had his forelegs planted wide and his head down gulping great draughts of the clear water. Pablos was a little upstream of the bull, cupping his hands and drinking eagerly. Zirza joined him. When they had slaked their thirst Zirza dipped her face in the water and washed it with her hands.

"It smarts with the salt water," she told Pablos. Their faces were indeed caked with salt and Pablos followed her example and washed too.

Above the banks of the stream was a narrow valley of sweet lush grass. Niro began grazing.

"I wish we could live on grass too," Pablos said. "I'm hungry."

"So am I," said Zirza. "What shall we do?" She seemed to put all her trust in Pablos.

"We must go and find food somewhere. We won't get anything just by sitting here."

Pablos rose and chased after Niro. "Come here, Niro!" he called. Niro was reluctant to leave his patch of grass but he turned obediently towards Pablos as a dog would have done. Pablos took hold of the halter and they climbed up the valley by way of a shallow gorge. At the top of the gorge they came out on a low hill. Pablos shaded his eyes with his hand and surveyed the country before them.

The land rose steeply from the banks of the little river to mountains in the south and the west. The mountainsides were clad in dark forests of cypress trees, but on the slope immediately before them were olive trees, the branches heavy with olives. There were carob-bean trees too, almond trees bearing nuts, and straggling wild vines with grapes already ripening.

Pablos tethered Niro to an old olive tree so that he could not stray and the children gathered fruit from the lower branches of the trees. They crammed olives, beans and grapes into their mouths till their lips and chins were all stained with the juice.

"Stop eating now!" Pablos ordered suddenly. "If we take too much we'll be sick. Let's crack a few nuts instead and eat those slowly."

He climbed into an almond tree and shook down some nuts, which Zirza gathered. Then they sat on a rock and broke the shells with a piece of stone. As they chewed the nuts they looked towards the sea. Though the waves were still flecked with white they were not so huge and the sea was no longer so menacing.

"I can't see any wreckage from the ship," Pablos remarked. "We were lucky to escape with our lives."

"This is a lot better than the ship. I wouldn't mind staying here," Zirza said. "I can see caves among those rocks which might shelter us." She waved her hand towards an outcrop of rock higher up the hill which had several dark cave mouths.

Pablos turned and looked at them too. "Yes, we could live there for a time," he agreed. "But we'll need other food besides berries and nuts. When winter comes there won't be any left on the trees."

"Perhaps we could stay here till winter," Zirza said. "It would never be really cold here."

"There'll be rain later in the year and a cold wind from the north. No, we must look for a place where there are houses and people."

"People? Fierce cruel men?" Zirza shuddered. "I hate men like those pirates. Besides, I don't want to be a slave and be beaten."

"I don't want to be a slave either," Pablos told her. "But not all slave masters are cruel. It would be better to be a slave to a good master than to die of hunger in winter."

"I still don't want to be a slave. Suppose different masters took us? I don't want to be separated from you now, Pablos. You're like a brother to me."

"I never had a sister," Pablos said thoughtfully. "But if I had I'd have liked her to be like you."

Zirza looked pleased. Pablos went on, "All the same we must find people and shelter. But I promise you, Zirza, that I'll fight to keep you and Niro with me. I won't let anyone separate us if I can help it. Now let's climb the hill and see what lies beyond."

"Let's look at that cave up there as we go. It might shelter us for a while." Zirza still thought she would rather live wild among the hills than find shelter as a slave.

To please her Pablos picked up Niro's tether and urged him up the slope towards the cave. Laurel bushes stood near the entrance. As they drew level with it Pablos's sharp eyes saw a pathway of beaten earth leading to it from over the hill.

"Look! There's a path! Men must have made it."

"It could have been made by goats. There are wild goats up on those crags." Zirza pointed to a little group of goats near the top of the hill.

Pablos was not convinced. "They may not be wild. They may belong to a farmer."

Before the cave stood a fig tree. Pablos gathered a handful of figs for both of them. Then they stopped with one accord at the dark entrance to the cave. Zirza felt just a bit afraid.

"You stop here with Niro and I'll take a look inside," Pablos suggested. "Lie down, Niro."

Niro obeyed and Pablos took a few steps inside the cave, then waited till his eyes got used to the darkness. In the gloom he thought he could make out something white. He put out a hand and groped towards it. It was a white pillar rising to the roof of the cave. Though he did not know it the pillar was a stalagmite, made by the constant dripping of water through the cave roof to the floor below, where it left a speck of limestone with every drip. It had taken hundreds, maybe thousands of years for the limestone pillar to grow.

Suddenly, when he was within a yard of it, Pablos stumbled among some objects on the floor. There was a clatter and something broke. Pablos picked it up.

"Are you all right, Pablos?" Zirza cried.

"Yes. I'm coming out again."

When he reached the cave entrance Pablos looked at the broken object in his hands. It was a pottery cup with a handle, orange in colour with black stripes, smudged at the edges as though the cup had been polished while the stripes were still wet. Pablos looked at it with astonishment.

"It's a cup, a beautiful cup!" he exclaimed. Then, with awe, "It's like the cups that people use to make offerings to the gods, or to bury with the dead. It's different from the cups we used at Corinth, much more beautiful."

"Are there dead people in there?" Zirza sounded a little frightened.

"I couldn't see any bodies unless they were at the back of the cave. It's too dark. There's a kind of white pillar with more cups round it."

Zirza's curiosity overcame her fear. "I'm going inside to see what I can find. Come with me."

With Pablos's help she groped her way towards the pillar and felt about at the foot of it. She came up with a small bronze jug. "Look at this!" she cried. "There are other treasures too."

Pablos was beginning to feel uneasy. "Don't take any more. I—I think this is a shrine to some god. People may come to the shrine and be angry if they see us taking things away. Come out! We must find some other place. Put the jug back."

"I want to keep the little jug. It's so beautiful."

"No, no! It's been given to a god. If we're found with it we might be put to death as thieves. Put it back, Zirza," Pablos pleaded.

With reluctance Zirza replaced the bronze jug among the pile of offerings and Pablos also restored the halves of the broken cup.

"Now we'll go and look for some other shelter or some kind person who'll give us a crust of bread," Pablos decided.

They had only taken a few steps out of the cave when they heard angry shouts and two men came pounding round the hillside towards them.

"What are you doing here? Thieves! Thieves in the holy place!" they shouted. They spoke a tongue similar to the speech of Corinth but rougher. Pablos was able to understand the word 'thieves', however.

"We aren't thieves!" he cried indignantly. "We're only looking for shelter."

"Search them! See what they've stolen."

Rough hands seized them and tugged at the tattered remnants of their clothing. Zirza burst into tears.

"Leave her alone! She hasn't done anything wrong," Pablos shouted furiously.

The man gave Pablos a blow which sent him staggering to the ground. As he struggled to rise Pablos clenched his fists angrily.

"Have you found any of the gifts to the goddess on them?" the other man asked.

Pablos's captor shook his head. "Perhaps they didn't have time to steal them before we came."

"We could have stolen the offerings but we didn't," Pablos said boldly. "All we were looking for was a shelter after being in the sea."

"In the sea? What were you doing in the sea?"

"Our ship was wrecked and we swam ashore."

"You *swam*?" The first man stared at him unbelieving.

"Yes, we were helped by my bull."

"Your *bull*!" Again the man looked at Pablos as if he were telling a lie. "Where is your bull then?"

Pablos stared around them. Where *was* Niro? He called the bull desperately. "Niro! Niro!"

From behind a thicket fifty yards away the head and horns of the bull appeared.

"There he is!" Zirza cried, pointing.

"Niro! Niro! Come here!" Pablos shouted desperately.

The bull came ambling towards them. Surprised, the man who was holding Pablos released him. He cried, astonished, "It is a bull! A young black bull! I've never seen such a black bull before."

"My master intended him as a gift to the god Zeus. I've looked after him ever since he was born," Pablos said proudly. "He'll obey my commands."

"Whoever heard of an obedient bull that would obey commands?" Pablos's captor sneered unbelievingly.

"You saw him come when I called him."

"That was nothing! He might come for food."

"Watch this, then!" Pablos told them. "Kneel, Niro, and let me climb on to your back."

The bull knelt and Pablos mounted his back and sat astride. The two men stared at him astonished.

"Can he do other tricks?" the first man asked.

"These aren't *tricks*. I've trained him to obey my commands. If I told him to charge at you, he would."

The men looked startled and drew back a little, then the first man took the other aside and whispered in his ear.

"A bull like that might be worth a lot of money. Khani would reward us well if we took the bull to him. If he put the bull in the ring at Knossos, he might win a lot of money."

"Let's take the bull to Khani, then," the second man agreed.

"No, not by ourselves. The bull obeys the boy. He might not obey us. We'll have to take the children too." He turned to Pablos. "We'll take you to Khani, our master, who will give you shelter and food and house the bull too."

Pablos considered a minute, then descended from the bull's back. "Have we far to go?"

"Over the hill and into the valley beyond."

"Then the girl must ride the bull. She's still weary and sick." Somehow Pablos felt he must protect Zirza. They seemed to belong together.

"Get on Niro's back," he told Zirza. "Kneel, Niro!"

Since their battle with the sea Zirza had lost all her fear of Niro. She climbed on to his back obediently and held his horns. Niro knelt placidly while she did so. Again the two men exchanged meaning glances.

"The children could also be worth money at the Bull Games at Knossos," the first man said in a low voice. "When we get near to Khani's house, I'll go ahead and tell the master what we've found."

They walked at a gentle pace over the hill and down into the valley beyond, Pablos leading the bull by his halter. The road followed the flank of a mountain which descended sharply towards the sea. Before long they had reached shore level again. Pablos looked seaward and saw a small island shaped like a dragon. He pointed towards it. "What island is that?"

"The island of Dia," the first of the two men replied a little impatiently. "Can't you urge your bull a little faster?"

Pablos made a clicking noise with his tongue and teeth and Niro lifted his hoofs a little quicker. The path swung round a wide curve flanking the sandy bay. A stone mole jutted out into the bay and ships were beached beneath its shelter. Suddenly, round a bend in the road, a fine mansion of two floors stood before them.

"It—it's like a palace!" Pablos cried. "Who lives there?"

"Khani, our master," the first man said with respect. "We're taking you to him."

"Who is Khani?" Pablos asked. "Is he the king of this land?"

"No, he's not the king but he ranks high at the King's court. He's a priest and a great merchant too."

"How can he be both?" Pablos was puzzled.

"He deals in the things sacred to our religion: double

axes, lamps, altars and fine vases. He sends them in ships to other lands beyond the sea. He's a great and rich man and you must treat him with respect and bow low in his presence," the man warned Pablos.

Pablos tossed his head slightly. "I'm not his slave."

"Not yet, but you will be," the second man sneered at him.

Pablos felt uneasy. So he and Zirza were to be slaves—perhaps to a master who would beat and starve them? Then he stiffened. "We shall see about that," he told the man in a proud voice.

4 At the House of Khani

The men turned in at a large wooden gate which was opened for them by a black boy. A road paved with large stone slabs led towards an archway with double wooden doors. Maron, the elder of their captors, spoke to a sentry holding a double-headed bronze axe and he flung open the doors for them.

"Go, now, and tell the master," Maron said to the second man.

Pablos hesitated with the bull's halter in his hand. The doors, beautifully inlaid with different coloured woods, opened on to a small square courtyard. On the south side of the court stood a large pair of curved horns like those of a huge ox, mounted on a pillar of stone. The walls were decorated with frescoes, brightly coloured paintings on plaster, of lilies and reeds with palm trees. One wall had wavy lines of blue to represent the sea and amidst the waves were dolphins and octopuses playing among shells.

Pablos stood in the entrance, staring. Even his master at Corinth had not got a house like this! Zirza was still sitting on the bull's back. "Oh! Oh, it's beautiful!" she cried. "Are we going to live here?"

Four doors, all open, led into another paved court and from this inner court came a tall man. He had a princely and commanding air and Maron and his companion bowed low before him.

The upper half of his body was bare, showing strong muscles. Two gold bracelets enclosed his wrists, one bearing a large seal of ivory engraved with a lion springing at a dog. His wide belt was studded with pearl shell and gold discs and below it he wore a blue garment almost like a short skirt ornamented with bands of gold embroidery. He was such a magnificent figure that Pablos cried out, "He must be a god!"

Maron's hand pressed his shoulder. "He is our master, Khani," he whispered in Pablos's ear. "Bow before him."

The two men bowed low, their heads almost touching the ground. Pablos hesitated, then followed their example. He had a sudden inspiration. "Hang on to Niro's horns," he whispered to Zirza, then gave a brief command to Niro. "Lower your head!"

As Khani approached the group it looked as if Pablos, Zirza and the bull were all bowing to him together. Khani was astonished. "Who are these?" he asked Maron.

"The children Mentos brought you word of, sir. We found them near the cave."

"And the bull?"

"The boy says it's his and that the bull carried them through the sea when their ship was wrecked."

"I have never seen an all black bull before," Khani said, his eyes wide with surprise. "Come here, lad, and tell me how that bull comes to be yours."

Pablos put the bull's halter into Zirza's hands and approached Khani. There was something about Khani that commanded respect and trust, and his eyes were kind. Pablos found he could talk to him easily and he poured out the story of his capture by the pirates and the storm that had wrecked their ship. Khani listened patiently, putting in a question now and again. When Pablos had finished he asked, "And what will you do now, boy?"

"I am looking for a home for myself and my sister." Pablos threw a quick glance at Zirza. "A good home where we'll be well treated and where there's a pasture for my bull."

Khani smiled. "Suppose I promised you and your sister a home, would you give me your bull?"

Pablos was well aware that Khani could force him to give up the bull but he did not let that show in his face. He decided to bargain bravely.

"No, I won't be parted from my bull," he answered, facing up to Khani. "But we might *both* be willing to work for you."

Again Khani smiled. "And how could your bull work for me? He's a very young bull, too young to breed."

Pablos remembered what Zirza had told him about the Bull Games at Knossos. He chanced a shot in the dark.

"He might do well in the Bull Sports that you hold on this island. And I have taught him obedience. He can do other things besides bowing to you and I could train him for you. He's a clever bull."

Khani liked the boy's fearlessness. "Where do you come from, boy?" he asked.

"From beyond the sea." Pablos pointed northwards. "We were carried off by pirates from my home at Corinth, I and the black bull and . . . my sister," he added.

Khani smiled at his hesitation. "For brother and sister you're not alike. You're fair-haired and blue-eyed and she's dark-haired and brown-eyed."

"My mother was from the far north," Pablos put in quickly. I . . . I am like my mother and Zirza's like her father," he made a guess.

Khani smiled again. "Perhaps you've *taken* her for your sister?"

Somehow Pablos could not lie to this quiet man who looked him so directly in the eyes. "Perhaps you're right," he parried. "But I mean to keep her as my sister and she must stay with me."

Khani was content with this answer. So the boy was truthful as well as fearless? His heart warmed to Pablos.

"That might be arranged," he agreed. "My wife could do with another handmaid. You would be well treated but you would have to work for us as slaves."

Pablos was a practical boy. He knew that Khani could take them as slaves without their consent. Even if Khani let them go free, where could he and Zirza and the bull find a home? They were powerless in a strange land. This man seemed to be a man of authority, a nobleman perhaps? He had a beautiful house. They might go much further and fare worse. Besides, he had a kind and honest face . . .

Zirza was looking from one to the other in mute bewilderment.

"Would you work for this nobleman's wife, the lady of the house?" Pablos asked her.

"Would you be here too?" she asked.

"We would all three be in this man's service, you and I and the bull."

"Then if you stay, I must stay too," Zirza decided.

Just then a woman came out of an inner court. She was tall and shapely with black eyes and hair that was cut square in a fringe on her forehead and fell behind her head in twisted curls to her shoulders. She was richly dressed in a dark orange-sleeved bodice, laced up the front with gold thread, but open at the breasts as was the fashion with all the ladies of Crete. The bodice was tucked into a broad silver belt. Below the belt was a skirt of purple silk in tiers of flounces. From the belt too there hung a white apron embroidered in a check design. Silver bracelets jangled on

44

her arms. Zirza's eyes opened wide. She had never seen anyone so splendidly attired.

"Who are these children, Khani?" the lady asked.

"Two castaways thrown up by the sea. They will belong to us now, Amaltha, a waiting-maid for you and a herd-boy for me."

Amaltha sniffed with disdain as she looked Zirza over. "She is a very dirty child," she said. Zirza's clothes were streaked with sand and mud and her hair was hanging in matted rat-tails. "I don't know if I want her for a maid-servant," Amaltha said with a toss of her head.

Zirza's face flushed angrily and she might have answered sharply but Pablos gripped her wrist. "I'll speak for you," he muttered in her ear. He made a bow to Amaltha.

"My sister is not really a dirty child. We were both tossed into the sea and thrown upon the sand. If she could wash she would soon be clean again."

"Mmph!" Amaltha gave a little snort of disdain but she relented so far as to say, "Washed she will be! My women will pour ewers of water over her and then we shall see what she looks like."

Zirza gave a little shiver of fear but Khani's mouth was puckered into a smile as he looked at his wife. He was used to Amaltha's sudden flares of temper and regarded her indulgently as a petulant pretty child.

"That's settled, then. You take the girl to your women and give her clean garments," he said firmly to Amaltha.

Amaltha shrugged, but beckoned to Zirza. "Come with me."

With a pitiful backward glance at Pablos Zirza reluctantly followed her new mistress.

Khani looked the black bull over again. "He's a good animal. He should do well at the Bull Sports."

It was Pablos's turn to look troubled. "I've heard something of these Bull Sports but I'm not sure what happens."

"Acrobats run at the bull when he charges and grip him by the horns and turn somersaults over his back. The Bull Sports take place every full moon in the great Bull Ring at the Palace of Knossos. But your bull is only half-grown. It will be a little time before he is ready for the Sports."

Pablos gave a sigh of relief, then asked, "Where will my bull be kept?"

"There is a good dry byre for him behind the house."

"Niro has never been kept in a byre. Ever since he was born he has lived on the hillside with me. I don't think he would take kindly to a byre. He wouldn't grow as strong as he would if he roamed the hill pastures." Somehow in his care for Niro Pablos had forgotten all his fear of Khani and had even forgotten that he was now a slave at Khani's bidding.

Khani liked the way the boy spoke out. "I've no doubt there are many good hill pastures on my lands," he said dryly. "But if you were free to roam the hillsides with the bull you would have to give me your word that you would not run away."

Knowing that this man was willing to trust his word, Pablos felt a sudden surge of trust in return. "I promise that I and the bull will stay with you as long as you are our master."

"That is good," Khani said gravely. "Now follow me to the servants' quarters, where you and the bull will stay at night."

"Please, master, one other question," Pablos begged. "Will I be able to see my sister sometimes?"

For once Khani seemed a little doubtful. "She will be my

wife's servant and will have to obey her, but perhaps when the Lady Amaltha doesn't require her services she may be free to see you."

With that reply Pablos had to be content but secretly he was determined to see Zirza soon and make sure all was well with her.

Zirza had followed the Lady Amaltha to the women's quarters. They went down a long narrow corridor with doors to the right and left. Zirza caught glimpses of fine apartments on the right with painted frescoes on the walls. Amaltha put her head in at one door and a girl came running. Amaltha gave a sharp order then pushed Zirza round a turn in the corridor and out into a paved courtyard at the back of the building.

Trembling, Zirza waited in the courtyard. Then Amaltha returned, followed by a girl carrying a large ewer, which she filled from a well in the corner of the courtyard.

"Over there!" Amaltha ordered curtly and pointed to a stone trough. "Strip off those dirty rags and stand in the trough."

At first Zirza stood still, shocked and indignant.

"Do as you are told," Amaltha snapped.

Zirza began with trembling fingers to loosen the plaited girdle round her waist and to pull her linen garment over her head. Then, shivering, she stepped into the trough. An older waiting woman took the ewer from the girl and at a signal from Amaltha she poured the water over Zirza. The water was icy cold and Zirza let out a shriek of dismay. Shaking, she sank down in the trough.

"Another ewer of water, then wash her," Amaltha commanded.

This time Zirza was more prepared for the deluge and

hid her face under her arms. The waiting woman took a sponge and washed Zirza with it, then pulled her out of the trough and towelled her roughly with a long piece of coarse linen.

"Now her hair," Amaltha ordered. "Kneel down beside the trough, girl!"

Zirza hesitated but the woman whispered to her, "Do as you are told, child! It will be better for you."

Zirza knelt and the woman pushed the top of her head into the water and rubbed at her hair with the sponge. Then, at a word from her mistress she took a bone comb and tugged at Zirza's tangled locks. Again she whispered to Zirza, "Endure it, child! I daren't be too gentle. Hold your head up as though I'm giving you orders."

Zirza obeyed, clenching her teeth, though the tears started into her eyes.

"Well done!" the slave woman whispered encouragingly.

At last the cleansing was over and Amaltha inspected her.

"That will do," she said curtly. "Each day you will wash yourself at this trough before you wait on me." She turned to the waiting woman. "Take her down to the women's quarters and put a clean robe on her."

Zirza felt naked and ashamed as she followed the waiting woman. Amaltha disappeared through another door. Quickly the waiting woman folded the damp towelling round Zirza. "That will make you feel less ashamed," she said in a low voice. "Don't let the rough treatment upset you. We've all had to go through it, her woman slaves. She spares nobody."

"Does she . . . does she beat you?" Zirza faltered.

The woman shrugged. "Sometimes she strikes us. She

has a quick temper and she could order us to be whipped. Be sure and obey her instantly and give her no cause for anger. What's your name?"

"Zirza."

"That's an unusual name. You're not from this island?"

Zirza shook her head.

"From over the sea, then?"

"Yes. We were taken by pirates from the land near Corinth and the pirates' ship was wrecked but Pablos and I managed to swim ashore."

"Pablos?"

"My . . . my brother. Khani has taken him into his service. Will I be able to see him?"

The woman did not reply at once. She produced a single linen garment like a loose shirt and pulled it over Zirza's head. "It's possible you'll be able to see him but I wouldn't ask Amaltha about it if I were you," she said at last. "My name is Elena. If you're in any difficulty you can come to me. I too was taken from my home many years ago as a slave, so we'll stick together."

Elena adjusted a plaited leather girdle about Zirza's waist. "If you need a clean gown come to me for it. Never show yourself before my lady in a soiled dress or with dirty hands. She looks on it as an insult to herself. This room is where the women slaves eat and sleep. There's a stone bench along the wall with sheepskins. That will be your sleeping place, next to me, but don't appear to be too friendly with me when the other women come. They might carry tales to Amaltha."

"Thank you. I'll remember," Zirza promised. She felt she had found a friend.

"Have you eaten today?"

"Only berries from the bushes."

"Then take that bowl and go to the kitchen through that door. A servant will give you food. You'll find the other women slaves there already. Be friendly towards them but guard your tongue."

"Thank you, Elena." Zirza was grateful for her friendly help. She took the bowl and went through the door.

In the kitchen Zirza found half a dozen women standing round a table helping themselves from a huge platter over which an elderly crone presided. The old woman beckoned her forward.

"Are you the new slave?"

Zirza nodded.

"Did Elena send you in here?"

"Yes."

"Make way for the girl," the old woman directed. "Take what you want from the platter," she told Zirza.

On the platter were slices of boiled meat seasoned with herbs and some pieces of wholemeal bread. Zirza took two or three pieces of meat and a couple of crusts of bread and then looked round for a place to sit. There was a space on a wooden bench near the door. Zirza sat down next to a couple of young women.

"You should ask our permission to sit beside us," one of them told her coldly.

Zirza remembered Elena's warning and gave a meek answer. "I didn't know. I'm a new slave. May I sit here?"

The woman nodded curtly. Zirza sat down again and was just lifting a piece of meat from her bowl when the woman reproved her. "You've not given thanks to the Earth Mother for your food."

Zirza hastily set down her bowl and placed the palms of her hands together as she saw another woman doing and moved her lips as though in prayer. Then she looked at the other woman as if asking permission to eat. When the woman nodded, Zirza began to eat slowly, aware that several pairs of eyes were watching her. She was only half-way through her meal when the sound of wooden clappers echoed through the corridor. Immediately all six women set down their bowls and made for the door.

"What is it?" Zirza asked, clutching at the woman next to her but she just pushed Zirza out of the way. Elena appeared in the doorway.

"It's our mistress summoning us. Run with the others, child."

Zirza dropped her bowl and ran swiftly along the corridor after them. In a bunch they thrust themselves through the door into the Lady Amaltha's apartment. Amaltha lay on a couch draped with deer skins. She looked haughtily over her slaves, then beckoned to the woman who had sat next to Zirza.

"Make up my couch for the afternoon sleep, Zapphaeia. You, Elena, bring me a honey drink." She caught sight of Zirza behind Elena. "Oh, and you, new one! Bring me more pillows."

"In the cupboard in the next room," Elena hissed at Zirza as they hurried from the room together.

Zirza collected two pillows and returned to Amaltha's room. She stood before Amaltha, not knowing what to do.

"Don't stand there like a fool! Put the pillows behind my back!" Amaltha barked at her.

With nervous hands Zirza began to tuck the pillows behind Amaltha's shoulders. Suddenly Amaltha gave a cry of rage.

"Clumsy fool! You pulled my hair then!" She seized the pillow and flung it full in Zirza's face. It burst and a shower of feathers fell out.

"Get down on your hands and knees and pick up every feather," Amaltha commanded, her face dark with anger. "You, Zapphaeia, fetch another pillow."

Zirza began stuffing the feathers back into the pillow. When Zapphaeia returned Amaltha said, "Now show this stupid girl how to put the pillow behind my back."

Zapphaeia took her mistress's hair carefully and lifted the curls over the pillow which she put gently in place.

"Now finish picking up the feathers and get out of my sight!" Amaltha told Zirza. Zirza was only too glad to do so. On her way back to the women's room she met Elena carrying a cup of lemon juice and honey.

"Do *all* the women slaves have to run when the mistress claps the wooden boards together?" she ventured to ask.

"Always! Run quickly when you hear them even if it's the middle of the night. Sometimes Amaltha punishes the last one."

"I'll make sure I'm not last," Zirza said to herself, and later, thinking of how she would have to run at Amaltha's harsh bidding, day and night, she wept silently and secretly.

5 The Young Acrobats

Pablos and Zirza each entered into a new and separate life. Every morning Pablos took Niro to the hill pasture as he had done in Corinth and every evening he returned with the bull to the byre behind the house. There they slept on piles of hay. Pablos was well fed on goat's meat and cheese, and fruit was to be had for the picking. Now and again Khani came to inspect the bull.

"He'll make a fine bull when he's fully grown." Khani looked with approval at Niro. "You're doing well with him."

Pablos was pleased to stand well in Khani's eyes. Every day his esteem for his master grew. Every day, too, his love grew for his bull. On the quiet hillside Niro followed him about like a dog, took titbits of green plants and berries from his hands, and when Pablos rehearsed the tricks he had taught him, the bull seemed to enjoy them as much as Pablos. At Pablos's command he stood still, bowed his head, knelt and allowed Pablos to climb on to his back. Sometimes they would race together, bull and rider, along the hillside. Pablos taught Niro to leap over a little stream while carrying him. Sometimes they would swim together in a deep pool.

Though Pablos was happy in his companionship with the bull there was always in his mind a nagging ache for Zirza. Since she had disappeared into the women's quarters he had not been able to speak with her. Then, one day, from the shelter of a doorway leading into the court-yard a woman beckoned to him. It was Elena.

"You are Pablos?" she asked.

"Yes."

"I have a message from your sister."

"From Zirza? Is she well?" he asked eagerly.

"She's well in body but her spirits are low. She's sad because she hasn't been able to see you. We've heard that you stand well with Khani. She asks you to beg him to let her see you from time to time."

"Could she not ask the Lady Amaltha?"

Elena shook her head. "My lady will not grant favours, but she will obey any order my lord Khani gives. That's all. See what *you* can do. I mustn't be seen talking to you."

Elena scurried away to the women's quarters.

Pablos pondered the problem. Somehow he must approach Khani to ask for a measure of liberty for Zirza. How to do it? Perhaps if he could please Khani even more with the black bull? He worked harder than ever to teach Niro new tricks.

Maron had become his friend and had told him more about the Bull Sports at Knossos. Pablos began to wonder if he could train Niro to let him vault over his back. It might please Khani.

That very morning, while the dew still lay on the grass, Pablos led Niro to a small level area on the hillside. He commanded Niro to stand still and bend his head. This time, instead of climbing quietly on to the bull's back, he retreated a few paces, then ran at Niro as the bull faced him. He gripped Niro's horns and swung himself over the bull's head and sat astride, facing Niro's tail. Beyond shaking his head in surprise, Niro stood still. Pablos got down and rewarded him with a handful of grapes.

"Now we'll do it again," he said.

Pablos spent most of the morning perfecting this new

trick. Niro soon learned to expect the leap and braced his forefeet as Pablos gripped his horns.

Pablos spent a day or two on this acrobatic exercise, always rewarding Niro with a handful of sweet grapes or berries.

"But I end up on Niro's back, facing his tail!" Pablos said to himself. "That won't do if I want to ride him. I must try to turn in the leap."

The next time he leaped higher, twisted his hands on the horns, flung his whole body in the air, turned sideways and came down facing Niro's head. Niro turned his head, a questioning look in his eyes, but he stood like a rock.

"Good! Good!" Pablos patted his shoulder. "You're a clever bull, Niro. We'll try it again."

For several days Pablos tried variations of the leap, twisting sideways, even doing a somersault over Niro's tail to land on the ground. Beyond an anxious turn of the head to make sure Pablos was still there, Niro did not budge.

"Now I must teach you to run at me as though you're going to charge me but to stop when I grip your horns."

Pablos ordered Niro to stand still and he retired about fifty paces from the bull.

"Now, come, Niro!" he cried and beckoned with his hand.

Niro came careering happily towards him. Pablos ran to meet him mid-way, gripped his horns and vaulted over his back. This was a new game for Niro and he liked it. After two or three tries he naturally put his head down on the approach as though he was really charging the boy and almost scooped Pablos up on his horns and over his back. Both Pablos and the bull had complete trust in each other.

All this time Pablos had no chance to speak to Khani

about Zirza. Then, one morning as Pablos was going through his vaulting tricks Khani appeared on the hillside pasture. He watched the boy and the bull closely. Pablos did not see him at first; he was so absorbed in timing his tricks exactly with Niro. When they both stopped for a breather and for Pablos to reward Niro with a handful of grapes, Khani approached them.

"Have *you* taught the bull those tricks, Pablos? You alone?"

"Yes. Niro's never had any other herd-boy. I had him right from birth when his mother died."

"He doesn't seem to mind when you leap on his back."

"No. You've seen him. I think he rather enjoys it."

Khani looked thoughtful. "Would he let any other person vault over him like that?"

Pablos pursed his lips doubtfully. "I don't think so. You see, he *knows* me. Before he would accept anyone else he would have to know them." A sudden inspiration came to him. "He knows Zirza ... my sister. He might allow her to leap on his back too."

"You think so?"

Pablos nodded. "But Zirza is now a servant in the women's quarters. I haven't seen her since we came here. If Zirza could be free to come to the hillside I might train Niro with her too."

Khani smiled. "That might be arranged. But tell me, is Zirza really your sister?"

Pablos felt he could not lie to Khani. "I took her for my sister when we were both carried off by pirates." He told Khani how he had found Zirza on the pirate ship.

Khani listened gravely. "I make no promises that Zirza will join you on the hillside but I will see what can be done." He gave Niro a pat on his flank and went away down the hill again but he left Pablos with a flicker of hope.

Khani made his way to Amaltha's apartment. Zirza was there combing Amaltha's hair and arranging it in long ringlets. She was just finishing her task.

"You can go now," Amaltha told her.

Khani waited till Zirza had left the room, then asked, "Is that the new girl slave?"

"Yes."

"She dresses your hair well."

"Mm! Not badly! She's sullen, though, with never a smile, but I have taught her obedience."

"Has she seen her brother since she was your slave?"

"The bull herd-boy? No. I don't permit my women to mix with the men from the farm." Amaltha tossed her head.

"Pablos is hardly a man, yet," Khani commented. "He's clever with the bull, though." He described how he had watched Pablos vaulting. "That bull is a treasure. I'm thinking of putting him and Pablos in the Bull Sports at the King's Palace at Knossos."

Amaltha looked up sharply.

"They might be worth a lot to us in wagers," Khani said casually. "I understand his sister handles the bull well too. She might also be trained to the bull-leaping. A double act with Pablos and his sister would be very popular with the crowd, no doubt, and would please the King too. But then, the girl is *your* slave and you need her to dress your hair."

Amaltha frowned. "Well . . . " she began and hesitated.

"Don't trouble yourself about it. It was just an idea. Maybe, though, if the boy and his sister and the black bull do well at the Sports, the King might give me a gold chain which would look well looped round your hair," Khani said craftily. "But you need the girl to wait on you." He began to turn away.

"Wait!" Amaltha seized him by the wrist. "I would still want Zirza to arrange my hair. She does it better than the other women, but it doesn't occupy her all day. I could do without her in the morning, if she could be here to make me ready for the guests who join us in the evenings. She could go to her brother on the hill in the early morning."

Khani smiled to himself. "That seems a good arrangement."

"But it must be understood that if I need her for any special service she stays here and puts her duties to me first," Amaltha hastened to bargain.

"Oh, yes, of course!" Khani agreed. "Well, I'll leave you to tell the child she can see her brother." He thought it wiser not to make too much fuss about Zirza.

Amaltha summoned Zirza who came and stood with bent head and downcast eyes. She thought that once again she must have offended Amaltha and would be punished for it, though she could not think what she had done wrong. She had done her best to arrange Amaltha's hair prettily and this time Amaltha had not slapped her or thrown anything at her.

"You have a brother, a herd-boy?" Amaltha asked.

"Yes, mistress." Zirza wondered what was coming next. Had Pablos done anything wrong? Her heart gave a little jump of fear for him.

"He tends the black bull that my lord would like to show at the Bull Sports at Knossos?"

"Yes, mistress, so I have been told."

"It seems your brother could do with some help with

the bull. You are to be spared from my services to go to the hill pasture with him in the mornings."

Zirza lifted astonished radiant eyes to Amaltha. "You . . . you will let me go, my lady?"

Amaltha gave a peevish shrug of her shoulders. "Only on the condition that it does not affect your work for me. You are to be here to wait on me in the afternoon and to dress my hair for the evening. You understand that?"

"Yes, mistress," Zirza said meekly.

"You may go now," Amaltha said curtly.

Zirza skipped with joy on her way back to the women's quarters. Elena met her in the doorway.

"Why did the Lady Amaltha send for you? What's making you look so happy?"

"Oh, Elena, Elena! I'm to help Pablos with the bull in the mornings. I'm going to see Pablos again!"

"Who fixed that for you? My lord Khani? He was talking with our mistress before she summoned you."

"I don't know. All that matters is that my lady said I could go to see Pablos on the hill in the mornings but I'm to be on hand in the afternoons to arrange her hair when she wants me."

Elena frowned a little. "Be careful, then, Zirza. If it is Khani who's ordered it, my lady won't be too pleased. She'll be watching for an excuse to be angry with you. Don't give her one. Be very meek and obedient."

"I'll do my best," Zirza promised.

The next morning as Pablos drove Niro up the hill he heard a shout behind him. "Pablos! Pablos! Wait for me!"

It was Zirza. Pablos rushed to her, holding out his hands.

"Zirza! Zirza! I don't believe it! So Khani persuaded his lady to let you come?"

"I'm only to be free in the mornings. The rest of the day

and evening I must be ready to serve the Lady Amaltha."

"At least we have the mornings." Pablos held her at arms' length. "How thin and pale you've become, Zirza!"

"That's because I'm hardly ever in the sun. And I fretted because . . . because I couldn't see you and I didn't want to eat," Zirza stammered.

"We'll soon put that right. Every day I'll persuade Maron to give me enough food for two," Pablos promised her. "You've got to be well and strong for some purpose Khani has in mind."

"What's that?"

"I'm not sure yet. It's something to do with me and the bull and the Bull-Leaping Sports I think."

Zirza looked puzzled. "But why does he want me to help with the bull?"

"It isn't exactly 'help'," Pablos admitted. "He wants me to train you to do tricks with Niro."

Zirza gave a doubtful shake of her head, but Pablos took her hand. "Listen, Zirza. Some day it may be a help to us both. I won't ask you to do anything for a while, just to watch me and Niro."

"And if, after that, I don't want to learn tricks . . .?" Zirza hesitated.

"We'll wait and see, but please try, Zirza. If you don't, then Amaltha may refuse to let you come to the hill again. I don't want that to happen."

Zirza gave him a shy look. "Have you missed me, Pablos? You wanted to see me?"

"Of course!" Pablos said briskly. "Haven't I taken you for my sister?"

At the word 'sister' a shadow of disappointment crossed Zirza's face.

"Now sit in the shade of that bush and watch what I can do with Niro," Pablos told her.

He put the bull through his paces and Niro obeyed every command exactly. The bull seemed to know he had an audience. When Pablos did a double somersault over the bull's back Zirza clapped her hands.

"Come here and give Niro his reward," Pablos called to her.

Zirza gave Niro the handful of sweet grapes and the bull accepted it.

"He'll get used to you again if you reward him every day," Pablos decided. "Tomorrow I'll hoist you on to his back and lead him round the pasture. He's carried you before. I want him to get used to it again. Then, later, I'll show you how to leap on to his back."

"I wonder if I'll ever do that?"

"Yes, if you make up your mind to it. But every day I want you to practise running and leaping and turning somersaults by yourself on the ground so that your muscles will grow strong. Promise me you'll do that."

"I promise," Zirza said. Somehow Pablos gave her confidence and new hope of freedom.

Elena met her at the door as she returned from the pasture.

"You saw Pablos?"

Zirza poured out her happy news. She told Elena about Pablos's acrobatic feats on the bull and added, "Pablos wants to teach me to leap on to Niro too."

Elena narrowed her eyes. "So *that*'s why the Lady Amaltha let you go so easily? Be very careful, Zirza! Don't be too eager to sport with the bull."

"But Niro is good-natured and knows us both. I don't think Pablos would let me do anything dangerous.

Besides, I give Niro his reward after the exercise. He gets a handful of grapes. He loves sweet things."

"He does, does he?" Elena smiled a little. "We might do something about that to make sure Niro likes you even better."

"What will you do?"

"Wait and see! But come to me before you go to the pasture tomorrow."

The next morning Elena produced three small cakes from the pocket of her flounced skirt. "Here are three honey cakes, one for you, one for Pablos and one for Niro. It's a lucky thing that the Lady Amaltha put me in charge of her kitchen, but tell nobody except Pablos that I've given the honey cakes to you or you'll get us both into trouble with Amaltha."

"Oh, Elena, thank you!" Zirza gave her a hug. "I won't tell anyone."

"I thought of one other thing in the night. Your loose linen robe isn't suitable for bull-leaping. Its folds might get caught in the bull's horns or fly over your head so you couldn't see."

"What shall I do, then?"

"You must dress as a boy. At Knossos the girls who take part in the Bull Sports dress like the boys. It's safer and more seemly."

"But where will I get boys' clothing?" Zirza looked troubled.

"Leave that to me. Maron is a friend of mine. He has a son about your size. But no bull-leaping, mind, till you have the right clothes for it."

"I'll tell Pablos what you say," Zirza promised.

Pablos agreed with Elena. "She's right. Niro might not like it if his head was suddenly enveloped in white linen.

You'll jump more freely, too, in clothes like mine. I won't let you leap on the bull till you have boys' clothes. Today I'll just hoist you on to his back and let you ride him round the hill."

After Pablos had gone through his exercises with the bull, he helped Zirza to climb on to Niro's back and with Pablos leading Niro by a short rope they walked happily round the meadow. Then, when Zirza dismounted, she held out the honey cake to Niro who first sniffed at the strange smell, then took the cake gingerly in his mouth. Once he had tasted it, however, he licked his tongue round it with delight.

"He likes it!" Pablos exclaimed. "You must be the only one to give him the cake, Zirza, then he'll know that he only gets a nice titbit when you've done a trick with him."

The next day Elena beckoned Zirza into a side room. She produced a small bundle from the pocket beneath her apron. "There! From Maron. Your boys' clothes for the bull-leaping."

Zirza looked at the tiny bundle in surprise. There was a pair of very brief trunks, with a tiny side-panel, a wide embroidered belt and a short dagger to fit into the belt.

"Is that all?" Zirza looked slightly dismayed.

"That's all a boy wears, all that Pablos wears, and you must look alike. Slip on the little breeches now and fasten them at the waist with the belt."

The panel of the breeches was draped slightly over her left hip where the dagger went into a slot in the belt. The belt fitted tightly to Zirza's narrow waist.

"That is a good fit," Elena approved. "The upper half of your body and arms will be bare. You're slim so you'll look like a boy. It's the fashion, too, at the Court of Knossos for the ladies to leave their breasts bare, so you won't be alone in that. Now, slip your white robe over the top to go to the hillside and take it off when Pablos is ready to teach you the bull-leaping."

That morning when Pablos had finished his exercises on the bull and they were taking a rest, Zirza flung off her white robe. Pablos looked at her with admiration. "Now you're ready for the bull-leaping. You look just right for it. You're so slim and so light on your feet."

There was no doubt: Zirza was beautiful.

"We'll waste no time. I'll begin teaching you at once. You mustn't be afraid. This may be the way to win our freedom. It has already given you the freedom to come to the pasture with me. If we're to hold on to that chance to be together, then we mustn't disappoint Khani at the Bull Sports."

Zirza understood at once. She faced Pablos courageously. "Let's begin the lessons, then," she said a little shakily. "I'll do my best, but be patient with me."

"We'll begin by teaching you to vault over Niro's horns," Pablos decided. "Can you do a handspring and somersault like this?"

Zirza immediately copied him, light as a butterfly. The regular exercises had developed her muscles and sense of balance.

"That's good," Pablos said. "Now *I'll* do the same thing over Niro's horns." He ordered the bull to stand still with his head down.

Niro did not hesitate but bent his horns towards Pablos who seized them and swung himself nimbly head over heels on to Niro's back, then slipped to the ground again.

"Now, you!" he told Zirza. "Stand still, Niro! Head down!"

Niro obeyed, expecting Pablos to repeat his performance, but it was Zirza who took a sharp breath, jumped towards him, seized his horns and tumbled head over heels on to his back and slipped forward over his tail. Pablos caught her as she came off the bull's back. He let his own breath go in a sigh of relief. Only he knew how afraid he had been for Zirza as she launched herself towards those sharp curving horns. Niro had seemed to accept her but Pablos had to make sure.

"Dare you try it a second time?" he asked Zirza.

"Now I've done it once I'm not so frightened," she told him.

"Then give him only *half* his honey cake now, so that he knows it's you when you leap over him. You can give him the other half when you've done it a second time."

Niro champed his jaws with satisfaction over the tasty honey cake.

"Now, when I give the commands, you repeat them after me," Pablos told Zirza. "He must get used to your voice giving him instructions too."

Zirza called out the orders after Pablos.

"*Now!*" Pablos commanded.

Unhesitatingly this time Zirza seized Niro by the horns and swung herself over them and on to his back. Niro gave a quick bellow of surprise, but he stood quite still.

"Well done!" Pablos cried. "You stayed on his back this time. Try it a third time, then that'll be enough for today."

Zirza again accomplished the leap, then she gave Niro the rest of the honey cake and stroked his head while he chewed it.

"He's beginning to learn that you belong with us," Pablos said. "We three make a team now."

Zirza felt a warm, comforting feeling at the thought that the three of them belonged together.

Day by day the lessons continued. Always they began with limbering-up exercises for both of them: running, leaping and turning handsprings and somersaults before they pratcised on Niro. Zirza soon grew as agile as Pablos and though she had not the same strength in her arms, her body was lighter than his and she swung herself easily over Niro's horns. Niro learned to listen for her voice as well as that of Pablos, and it was quite a step forward when she gave her commands alone and Niro obeyed them. She learned to turn a second somersault on Niro's back after she had vaulted over his horns, to twist sideways and, with her hands clutching his horns, to lean forward and ride him like a jockey. Soon she was as fearless as Pablos, perhaps even more fearless, for Pablos always had a secret worry that something might happen to Zirza.

Then, one day while Pablos was putting Zirza through her paces, a figure appeared on the hill. It was Khani come to watch them. For a few minutes they did not know he was there. It was only after Zirza had done a somersault and stood on her hands on the bull's back that Khani spoke.

"That's excellent," he said, clapping his hands.

Though Pablos was pleased at his master's praise, a little shiver of apprehension ran down his spine. What was to come next? He soon knew.

"I think you're nearly ready for the Bull Sports at Knossos," Khani said. "Run back now to serve your mistress, girl. I want to talk to Pablos."

6 Knossos

When Zirza had disappeared round the hill, Khani turned to Pablos. "Do you think that you and the girl and the bull could perform your acrobatic leaps before a crowd in the great arena at Knossos?" he asked.

Pablos hesitated. "Niro has never performed before a crowd or in an arena. I don't know how he would behave there. Seeing so many people might upset him."

"We would have to take a chance on that," Khani said lightly.

"*I* would be prepared to take the chance with him *alone* but I wouldn't want to risk Zirza being hurt," Pablos replied.

"You think a lot of your . . . er . . . sister," Khani smiled, "but the two of you together with the black bull could win a lot of favour for me with the King. I agree that it might be a good idea to let the bull get used to crowds first though."

Pablos clutched at this straw. "Perhaps if he could get used to crowds before . . . before Knossos?" he faltered.

"That might be done. How would it be if you began by performing before some of my friends and the household and farm slaves?" Khani suggested. "We could see then how the bull reacts."

"Yes, that would be a good plan," Pablos agreed. He was eager to please Khani, who was a good master, and he was well aware that Khani could *order* them to appear at Knossos, whether they agreed or not. Besides, secretly

Pablos wanted to see Knossos for himself. He had heard such tales of its wonders from Maron and the other slaves.

"You think Nirou Khani is a palace but wait till you have seen Knossos," Maron had said. "Knossos is *splendid*, the most wonderful palace in the world."

Pablos thought, too, that perhaps at Knossos he might hear something that would help them in the future if they ever needed to make an escape. He knew Zirza was not happy with Amaltha and that she longed for freedom.

"If the bull behaves well in front of crowds, would you be happy for your sister to perform too?" Khani asked.

Pablos thought for a minute. At last he said, "Yes." Zirza might find greater freedom at Knossos from Amaltha's yoke. Then suddenly he put a plea to Khani. "You wouldn't ask my sister to leap any other bull than Niro? She's used only to Niro." Pablos had heard from Maron of the fierce bulls at Knossos and of the many acrobats who had died on their horns.

Khani knew of that too. He had no wish to lose either of his promising pair of acrobats in their early performances at Knossos. If the question of other bulls came up there would be time to deal with that later. For a season the crowds would be sufficiently delighted with the children on the black bull.

"I give you my word that Zirza won't be asked to ride or leap any bull but the black one, if it's against her own wishes," Khani promised, and Pablos was content with that.

From that time on a small audience would gather on the hillside to watch the children do their acrobatic tricks with the bull. Then Khani had an area fenced off near his house and Pablos took the bull down there and the delighted slaves watched the performance over the low fence. Amaltha heard whispers from her women of what was going on.

"It's said that Zirza is the child of a witch and she has witchcraft herself to bewitch the black bull," one woman told her. "She holds the bull in her power by the cake that she gives him when he's done well."

"Cake? What cake?" Amaltha asked sharply.

"Perhaps Elena could tell you," the woman said. She bore a grudge against Elena because Amaltha treated her better than the other slaves.

Amaltha sent for Elena. "What's this I hear about you giving a cake to Zirza to take to the black bull?" she asked severely.

Elena faced her fearlessly. "It's only a little honey cake such as your women eat. Besides, my lord Khani knows that Zirza gives it to the bull and he hasn't forbidden it."

She knew Amaltha would not wish to quarrel with Khani, who was master in his own house and who loaded Amaltha with jewels and presents when she pleased him.

"You should have asked my permission first," Amaltha said crossly.

"Yes, mistress, I should have done that." Elena pretended a meekness she did not feel. "Do I now have your permission to give Zirza the cake as usual?"

Amaltha did not want her meanness and spitefulness to reach Khani's ears. She knew that he set great store by the black bull and the slave-children who trained it and he would be angry at any interference.

"For the present you may, till I tell you to stop," she said haughtily to Elena. "Now get out of my sight and go back to the kitchen."

The next day, when Elena gave Zirza the honey cake,

she told her, "Amaltha knows about the cake and she's angry that I've been giving it to you. She might stop it suddenly. You must get the black bull to take other sweet things. It won't do to rely only on the honey cake. One day, perhaps when you perform at Knossos, it might be withdrawn."

"What can I give Niro instead? He loves the honey cake," Zirza said, dismayed.

"Here in this jar is a section of honeycomb with the honey dripping from it. Dip a piece of bread in the honey and give it to the bull, but don't do it yet. I'll keep on giving you the honey cakes till Amaltha stops them, which I'm sure she'll do when the chance comes. Meantime, let Pablos keep the honey for you."

"But why should Amaltha refuse to let me have the honey cake? Why does she dislike me? I do my best to please her when I dress her hair." Zirza sounded bewildered.

"Amaltha is a jealous woman and she can't bear anyone else to stand well in Khani's eyes," Elena told Zirza. "Watch your step with her and with Khani, my child, and don't give cause for any of the other women to carry tittle-tattle to her."

"I'll be careful," Zirza promised Elena.

Not long afterwards Khani was holding a party for his friends. He told Amaltha that he had decided to entertain them with the children's performance on the black bull. Amaltha pretended to be delighted and clapped her hands.

"That will indeed be a new entertainment. I would like to come along too, with the ladies who will be our guests."

"Very well. Maron will arrange seats for you all," Khani agreed.

70

"I'll wear my prettiest bracelets," Amaltha told him.

When the day of the party came, Zirza dressed Amaltha's hair with special care and wound chains of gold rosettes around it. For once Amaltha seemed pleased.

"I hear from my lord Khani that you are to perform on the black bull before our guests today," she said.

"Yes, my lady."

"I hope you will do your best to bring honour to my lord."

"I always try to please my lord Khani," Zirza assured her warmly.

"I'm sure you do. Today I shall be there with my guests to watch you do it."

There was a hint of jealousy in her voice which Zirza detected, and she remembered Elena's warning. "But why should Amaltha be jealous of a slave-girl?" Zirza wondered.

In the afternoon Pablos led the black bull with Zirza on his back into the grass enclosure. First Pablos did his leaps on to the bull with ease and confidence. Zirza followed him but she did not feel so happy with Amaltha looking on. She did not let her feelings show, however, and went through her routines with her usual coolness and assurance, bouncing lightly over Niro's back and even balancing on one foot with arms outstretched. Then she did a back somersault over Niro's tail and was caught by Pablos's ready hands. Khani's guests applauded loudly.

"These children are bull-leapers indeed," one man said. "Where did you get them and the bull, Khani?"

"From over the sea," Khani replied vaguely. His friends concluded that he had bought the animal and the young slaves on one of his many voyages, perhaps from Greece.

"You'll be showing them at the Bull Sports at Knossos, surely?"

Khani pretended to be uncertain. "Do you think they're good enough, Jason?"

"Indeed they are! I've never seen such a well-matched pair. The boy is fearless and the girl is a lovely child."

"Yes, she is very lovely," Khani agreed. "I look on them almost as if they were my own children."

Amaltha could hear what was said and her eyes flashed with anger and jealousy.

"I think our friends will have had enough of the show, my lord," she said quickly. "It's time we asked them to eat and drink with us."

She led the way towards Khani's apartment. They passed close to Pablos and Zirza. Khani clapped Pablos on the shoulder and patted Zirza's cheek. "You've done well, my children," he said, well pleased, but as Amaltha brushed past Zirza she hissed, "Get that absurd costume off at once and come and wait upon our guests."

Zirza had to hand dishes to the guests and to pour wine. She was tired but she did her best. She smiled charmingly when some of the guests praised her performance on the bull. All this added fuel to the flame of Amaltha's jealousy and she constantly scolded Zirza, calling her slow and careless. At one point she thrust out a foot secretly so that Zirza tripped over it and spilled some wine on the floor.

"Clumsy slave!" Amaltha cried and dealt Zirza a hard blow that sent her staggering to the ground. Even Khani took notice of this.

"Careful, wife! I don't want the girl injured if she's to perform at Knossos," he said sharply.

"Surely I have the right to reprove my servants when they are careless?" Amaltha retorted.

"The child is tired. Go to your bed, girl!" Khani ordered. Not even Amaltha dared to cross Khani when he gave commands in that tone, but her eyes followed Zirza venomously as she went through the door.

Zirza sought out Elena and wept in her arms. "Why does my lady hate me so?" she sobbed. "I've done my best to serve her and to please my lord Khani."

"Perhaps my lord has praised you too much in her hearing," Elena said shrewdly. "You did well at the bull-leaping, Zirza. Cheer up, child! Khani will want you to perform well at Knossos so he won't let Amaltha ill-treat you."

At last the day came when Khani and Amaltha and some slaves departed for Knossos. Amaltha was carried in a litter by four strong men but the rest of them set out to walk the dusty road of beaten earth. Pablos, with Niro carrying Zirza part of the way on his back, brought up the rear of the procession.

In the afternoon they rounded the flank of a mountain by a winding road which led down a gully to a wide bay. At the eastern end of the bay was the harbour of Amnisos with ships tied up at its long moles.

"That is the harbour that serves the Palace at Knossos," Maron told Pablos.

There were several well-built villas beside the road, some of them with two storeys and flat roofs.

"These are grand houses," Zirza said, her eyes wide with surprise. "I've never seen any like them before, except at Nirou Khani."

"Wait till you see Knossos!" Maron laughed.

They had not long to wait. After another couple of miles they crossed the stony bed of the Karaitos river. There was just a trickle of water there, for it was still the dry season. In a week or two the autumn rains would fill the channel with rushing torrents of water. At the mouth of the river was another small port, Katsamba. Now the road was paved by squared stones. As they turned a bend the great Palace of Knossos rose up before them on a huge mound. Pablos and Zirza stopped dead, catching their breath.

The Palace was immense: its shining white roofs stretched far to the west, topped by towers. It was not just one palace but a number of palaces linked to each other. Wide staircases led upwards from one floor to another. Great shafts, or light wells, took daylight to the lower floors. Pablos and Zirza could hardly believe their eyes.

"The King of this land must be a great man indeed!" Pablos declared.

"Our King is the greatest king in the world," Maron said proudly. "Thousands of slaves and servants work for him here. He has other palaces too, at Phaistos and Tamara, and his noblemen have fine houses, like Nirou Khani," he explained. "But Knossos is the richest of all. The King is lord, too, of all the seas around the island. His ships carry trade south to Egypt and north to Greece and the islands and even to the lands beyond the islands. Khani is one of the King's chief traders. He has many warehouses by the waterside but none are as big as these at Knossos. Here in the store-rooms are enormous jars, bigger than a man, that hold wine and olive oil, and wheat. There are other cellars with big chests that hold treasures of gold and silver and precious stones too."

Pablos's eyes grew bigger and bigger. "I should like to see these great store-rooms."

"I have a friend who looks after the oil and wine stores

and is in the King's favour," Maron said importantly. "Perhaps if you do well at the bull-leaping you will be well-liked by the Palace people and it might be arranged to let you see something of the Palace. Of course, you would not be allowed to see the jewel chests."

"And Zirza? Zirza would like to see the Palace too, wouldn't you, Zirza?"

Zirza nodded, her eyes shining.

"Well, she takes part in the bull-leaping too, so it might be permitted."

All this time they were plodding uphill. They turned westward along the north wall of the Palace towards the great north entrance, flanked by two high towers built of massive blocks of limestone. The men carrying Amaltha's litter entered a paved court and set her down there, just where the entrance narrowed between the pillars. The rest of Khani's small procession halted too.

"You must now join the women and follow them to the women's quarters," Maron advised Zirza. She slipped down from Niro's back but she lingered with Pablos.

"Where do I go with the bull?" Pablos asked Maron.

"We await Khani's command, then we go to the South East House where the King's noblemen stay when they come to Knossos. But first we have to go through the Central Court to be received by the King."

A ramp led to a great paved area with several wide stairways leading to the upper part of the Palace. All round the court were frescoes, paintings on plaster. Zirza exclaimed with delight at pictures of olive trees in flower, and one of a monkey gathering saffron in a garden. But what made Pablos catch his breath was a huge fresco of a bull, head down and red of eye, nostrils distended, making a furious charge.

"The Bull Sports!" he exclaimed.

"Yes, the Bull Sports are the King's great pleasure," Maron told him. "Look at the other wall over there."

This fresco showed a youth somersaulting over the back of a charging bull, while a young girl in boy's costume ran behind the bull to catch the boy as he leapt off the bull's back. The picture might have been one of himself and Zirza.

Pablos gave a little shiver. He and Zirza were safe so long as they only had to sport with Niro who knew them so well, but what if they were called upon to vault a strange bull? What might happen to Zirza who had grown so dear to him? Then he remembered Khani's promise and felt happier. Khani would not order Zirza to leap over any strange bull. As for himself, Pablos felt he could tackle any charging bull with the best of acrobats.

Great shields, shaped like a figure eight, hung on the walls where there were no frescoes, and long double-headed axes stood beside them. In the centre of the court was a stone pillar surmounted by a huge bull's head of stone, with tremendous curving horns.

As they passed through the great oblong court, twice as long on its east and west walls as it was on the north and south sides, Pablos and Zirza caught glimpses through the open doors of many chambers, the walls lined with paintings of lilies and birds and fishes. Everywhere, engraved on pillars and doors were the signs of the double-headed axe and the trident.

"What do those signs mean?" Pablos asked Maron.

"The double-headed axe is the symbol of our goddess the Earth Mother, Dhia," Maron explained.

"And that three-pronged sign?"

"That is the trident, the symbol of the Sea-God and it is

also the sign of our King, whose ships rule all the seas and trade in every part of the world," Maron said proudly.

Zirza took a quick peep into several of the rooms as they passed them. She saw servants handling beautiful vases and jugs with long spouts; elegant cups, all decorated with rosettes, bands and spiral designs in white on a dark surface. She longed to touch and handle them. Amaltha had vases and jugs too but none so beautiful as these. She hung behind to get a better look but Elena called her sharply.

"Hurry, child! Come along with the rest of us."

Zirza ran to join them.

"Why did you linger?" Elena asked in a low voice.

"The things in the rooms . . . the vases . . . they're more beautiful than anything I've ever seen."

"You'd better not let Amaltha hear you saying that. She's jealous of the Queen's treasures."

"Amaltha is jealous of so many things." Zirza tossed her head in disdain.

"Quiet, girl! Mind what you say! There are too many quick ears listening and too many quick tongues to carry careless words to Amaltha. Remember my warning."

"I will, Elena, oh, I will!" Zirza promised. She gave a quick sigh. "But those lovely vases . . . oh, if I could only touch them!"

"Do well at the bull-leaping and perhaps you might. The King's potter likes to watch the sport. A word in his ear and he might let you see his pottery. But hurry now! It would never do for us to fall too far behind Amaltha."

Khani and Amaltha had stopped before a short flight of four steps leading to a square room. Both of them bowed low before a very splendid figure standing at the head of the steps. It was the King. Everyone fell silent as he came forward. The King was tall with wide shoulders, curling black hair, dark eyes and proud, noble features. He wore a long draped loin-cloth of blue, trimmed with gold braid. His slender waist was encircled by a girdle set with gold rosettes and leaves. On his head he wore a cone-shaped hat into which were fixed many-coloured plumes of bright feathers. A bracelet of gold held his own particular seal round his wrist.

The King came down the steps and held out his hand graciously to Khani.

"It is good to see you here, Khani. I trust your sea-trade goes well."

"It does indeed, sire. I shall be bringing more tribute than ever from your ships this year."

"That is good news." The King extended his hand to Amaltha and raised her up. "Lady Amaltha, more beautiful than ever! I am glad you are able to come with Khani to our court."

Amaltha gave a little smirk of pride.

The King turned again to Khani. "But I hear that you have come to take part in our Sports and you have brought your own bull and bull team with you."

"By your leave, yes, sire," Khani replied.

"Is that your bull?" The King pointed to Niro. "I have never seen such a black bull before. His skin shines like ebony. And your acrobats? Where are they?"

Khani beckoned Pablos and Zirza forward.

"Kneel before the King," Maron hissed at Pablos as he passed.

Pablos fell on his knees at the foot of the steps, his hands upheld together. Zirza imitated him.

"They are very young," the King said in surprise. "Stand up and let me see you better."

The two children rose and stood obediently before him.

"Can you leap your bull?" he asked.

"Yes, my lord." Pablos spoke for both of them.

"They are very agile, sire," Khani told him.

"They come from other lands, surely?"

"Yes, sire, from the lands beyond the islands, from Corinth," Khani told him.

"You have done well to acquire two such young and beautiful slaves. This is a very pretty child." The King stroked Zirza lightly on the head. "It would be a pity if the bull injured her."

Amaltha stiffened when she heard the King's words and saw him touch Zirza. Her eyes sparkled angrily for a moment but she stored up the King's words in her mind.

"Niro, our bull, would never injure Zirza." Pablos spoke up boldly to reassure Zirza. "We are not afraid."

The King smiled at him. "Here is a brave young lad. Well, we shall watch you at the Sports in two days' time. Do well and you shall be granted favours." He turned to Khani. "We shall welcome you and Amaltha at supper tomorrow. We have a troupe of dancers coming from Rhodes."

Khani and Amaltha bowed low and the others followed their example. The King returned to his apartments and the little procession moved on to the long south corridor, around an elbow turn and came out at the South Gate with its towers. Here the party split and Khani, Amaltha and her women entered the Guest House while Maron led the men slaves to the west side of the Palace and the slaves' quarters. Here Pablos found a stable for himself and his bull next to the place where the royal bulls were kept.

Amaltha slept late next day and Zirza was able to find Pablos with Elena's help.

"It's a good thing I have you to guide me, Elena. I should be lost for ever in all these passages and court-yards," Zirza declared.

"I know the Palace of Knossos well. My mother and father were slaves here and I was brought up within its walls," Elena told her.

"How did you come to Nirou Khani then?" Zirza asked curiously.

"The old King gave me to Khani's father as a reward for good trade with Egypt. The Khani family have been good traders for several generations, but Khani has no son to carry on after him. But here's Pablos with the bull."

"I'm taking Niro to exercise in the great arena," Pablos told them. "Maron says it'll be quiet there just now. It's over there to the north-west beyond the West Court. I want Niro to get used to the ground before the Bull Sports. May Zirza come too, Elena?"

"Yes, for a short time. I'll come with you too, for we must be back soon and Zirza might never find her way alone."

The arena was deserted. Pablos looked at the tiers of seats cut in the sides of the small hill which encircled the arena.

"Do the onlookers sit there? If all those seats are occupied there must be hundreds of people."

"Most of the Palace workers attend the Sports," Elena told him. "There might be two thousand, the noblemen and their servants as well."

Pablos took a deep breath. "So many?"

"Yes. You won't be the only performers but you must

do your best to bring honour to my lord Khani and to earn the King's favour for yourselves."

"We shall do that." It was Zirza who spoke with great confidence. She had utter trust in Pablos and Niro. Luckily she did not know of Pablos's secret fear for her.

7   The Bull Sports

Pablos was given a straw bed in the quarters of the acrobats assembled for the Sports, but when all the others were asleep he crept out to be beside Niro. He was afraid strangers might handle his bull and he did not want Niro to be made nervous before the big performance. As soon as it was light he walked the bull quietly through the olive groves till they reached the shore. On a stretch of firm sand he exercised Niro and did one or two gymnastic feats. The waves were breaking on the shore with a dull booming sound. Pablos looked out to sea. There was no wind but there was a heavy swell which seemed to come from the sea-bed itself, as though the sea heaved uneasily. Down at the harbour the ships lifted and fell as they rode at anchor. Niro looked at the groaning sea and bellowed as if he feared it.

"It's all right, Niro. I'm not going to ask you to swim in the sea again," Pablos soothed him, stroking his head.

In the Palace too there was a kind of unease in the atmosphere. The air was sultry and close and the Palace servants went about their work in a lazy grumbling fashion. Animals whined miserably: the soothsayer who sat by the road leading to the sea kept looking over his shoulder fearfully and lifting his hands as if to ward off evil. Tempers were touchy and even the children quarrelled more than usual over their games.

Nowhere were tempers more uncertain than in the Guest House. Nothing could please Amaltha. She had her women running constantly here and there. Her scolding voice rose higher and higher. Zirza dressed her hair a dozen times and no arrangement pleased her.

"Clumsy creature! You tugged my hair with the comb then!" Amaltha turned and slapped Zirza hard across the face. Zirza struggled to hold back her tears. All day Amaltha had had her at her beck and call and she had not allowed Zirza to join Pablos in the morning. Zirza felt utterly weary and sad. It was at that moment that Khani came into the room. He saw the tears in Zirza's eyes, her one flaming cheek and the other deadly pale. He knew his wife's temper and he took in the situation at a glance.

"What? Zirza still here? It's time she was in bed if she's to do well at the Bull Sports tomorrow."

Amaltha threw Zirza a venomous look. "She is a stupid girl. She doesn't try to please me."

"Oh, mistress, I do . . ." Zirza could not stop the protest that rose to her lips.

Amaltha slapped her again on her other cheek.

"Enough, wife! To your bed, child!" Khani ordered, and when he spoke in that tone not even Amaltha dared to countermand him.

Zirza slipped quickly from the room. As soon as the door closed behind her Khani said coldly, "The girl is ready to drop with weariness. Surely, Amaltha, you have more sense than to keep her running about the way you do, knowing what she will have to do at the Bull Sports tomorrow?"

"She was my slave before she became your precious acrobat!" Amaltha answered angrily.

"Remember I gave her to you. If you treat her badly I will withdraw my gift."

Amaltha knew he might do this and she strove to

control her temper. Khani also thought the quarrel had gone far enough.

"I ask you only to be reasonable. I have a lot staked on the performance of these two young people and the black bull. You know how the King enjoys the Bull Sports. I want to please him. The King may even want to buy the bull from me. Who knows. But if he does, I'll be well rewarded, you may be sure."

Amaltha craftily grasped at this. "If he does, then you might be able to build a bathroom on to my apartments at Nirou Khani, like the one the Queen has here at Knossos!"

"That might well be," Khani agreed lightly. He knew how much Amaltha coveted such a bathroom. "But there must be no more hard work for Zirza until the Bull Sports are over. Is that understood? Everything depends on their performance."

Amaltha nodded sullenly. She knew she must agree.

The next day the crowds began to assemble early for the Sports. A heat-haze hung over the sea and there was a rumble of distant thunder. By early morning, however, the arena was crowded. Somehow the rumour had got around that there was to be an astonishing performance on a black bull by new young acrobats. Not only did the ordinary people throng Knossos but princes and their wives arrived from the Palaces of Phaistos, Mallia and Hagia Triada. The ladies were carried on litters. No nobleman's wife would dream of setting her feet on the dusty roads. They were elegantly attired in flounced dresses, open at the breast, and with embroidered aprons. There was a lot of competition for seats near the King's dais and most of the ladies staked their claims by putting down embroidered cushions on the hard stone seats.

Amaltha thrust her way forward to get as near to the King and Queen as possible. Beside her was the King's Treasurer, Kalamon, one of the mightiest and richest men on the island. Amaltha bowed graciously as she took the seat next to him and Khani sat on her other side.

Kalamon leaned forward to speak to Khani. "I hear you have a surprise new bull for us, Khani, and two young acrobats who have never performed in the Bull Sports before."

"That is so, my lord."

"Do you think they will do well?"

"They have practised very hard," Khani told him.

"Khani thinks they are wonderful," Amaltha remarked with a sarcastic sneer.

Khani looked sharply at his wife. "*I* did not say that. We will wait and see how they perform." His voice was cold.

Amaltha shrugged her shoulders. "They may do quite well on their *own* bull for they are used to him," she said lightly. Her words were not lost on Kalamon. It was his turn to give her a sharp glance.

Further conversation was drowned by the bellowing or the bulls as they were led from their byres. The sultry aif and the excitement of the crowds seemed to affect the bulls and they were more restive than usual.

Zirza stood beside Pablos, waiting. They were not to do their turn until three other teams of bull-leapers had performed. They watched a large bull being led into the arena and released. A team of four acrobats from Greece followed him. They danced round the bull, teasing him by darting in and giving him a poke in the ribs and performing antics in front of him.

"They're trying to provoke the bull," Pablos said.

'Look! He's pawing and stamping with one foot. They generally do that before they charge."

"Will . . . will the bull-leapers be hurt?" Zirza's voice trembled a little.

"No. He's an old bull. They'll be too quick for him and there are too many of them. He won't know which to attack first. Look! Here he comes!"

The bull made a sudden rush at the team leader but the youth had been expecting it and ran with outstretched hands, grasped the horns as the bull lowered his head and swung himself over the bull's head.

"Well done, Hippias!" Pablos shouted, but Zirza had gone rather pale.

The old bull soon tired and slank away to the side of the arena, unwilling to be the subject of their sport. Four acrobats were too many for him. There were shouts of derision and disgust from the audience.

"An old bull! Get rid of him! Kill him! Let him be sacrificed to Dhia."

"Is it your will that I kill him?" Hippias cried to the crowd.

"Yes, yes, kill him!" they shouted back.

Hippias took the short-bladed sword that he carried in his belt, ran to the bull and plunged the sword into the side of his neck. The blood gushed out and the bull sank to his knees his eyes glazing.

"Oh, the poor wretched animal!" Zirza cried with pity. "He stood no chance." A sudden fear choked her. "Oh, Pablos, they won't cry out for us to kill Niro, will they?"

Pablos stiffened, but he shook his head. "No, I could never do that." He looked at Zirza, who was trembling with fear for him too. "There will be no need. Niro will do all he's been trained to do and the crowd will be pleased.

They've seen blood shed already and perhaps now they'll be satisfied," he said in disgust.

The next performance went well but was not outstanding and the bull made his exit with the team when they had finished their act. Then the third bull was released into the arena. He was young and spirited and rushed madly round, pawing and snorting. Two acrobats, boys, stepped into the ring to torment him. One of them had a trident with which he goaded the bull from behind.

"There's no need to goad that one," Pablos said under his breath. "He's fierce enough already."

The leading acrobat managed a couple of leaps over the bull and his team-mate with the trident caught him cleverly as he vaulted over the bull's tail. All at once the bull sensed that his enemy was behind him and he swerved suddenly in his tracks, swung round and came at both of them standing together. The leader jumped aside but the one with the trident was not so quick. The bull rushed at him with his head on one side and the long pointed horn pierced the boy's chest. The bull lifted him and rushed in a mad circle round the arena, before tossing him off the horn and trampling on him. To Zirza's horror the crowd broke into a storm of applause.

"A noble bull! A bull indeed! Praise to the bull!"

The bull came to a standstill, dazed by all the noise. The team leader lifted his dagger. His face was very pale. "Is it your will that I should kill the bull?"

For once the spectators had had enough of blood. Besides, the bull had shown courage and cunning. He might provide them with more sport another day.

"No, no! Let him go free. Tomorrow he can fight again!" the mob shouted.

The team leader, still shaking with fear, went up to the

bull, caught hold of its short halter rope, spoke quietly to it and led the animal away.

"That's a brave lad," Pablos said, but Zirza was staring with horror at the body of the other youth which the arena slaves were carrying out.

"Oh, Pablos! Could that happen to us?"

Pablos had to reassure her quickly. It was their turn next.

"Of course not! Niro would never hurt either of us. He'll make little rushes at us but they'll all be in sport. You must grasp his horns as you've always done and vault on his back and dance. The crowd will *love* you. Khani, and perhaps the King too, will reward us. There'll be a piece of jewellery for you, I'm sure. It may be the way to earn our freedom."

Zirza took a deep breath. "I'll do my best," she said.

"Come on, then!" He signed to the attendant to open the doors into the arena and to let Niro enter.

The small black bull cantered to the centre of the arena and looked at the crowd who exclaimed at his beauty. Pablos had groomed his shining black coat till it was like polished ebony and he had polished the horns till they shone too. The bull stopped and looked round for Pablos.

"Go in doing your somersaults and handsprings," Pablos hissed in Zirza's ear.

For a moment they stood together at the entrance, small and beautiful, clad in white, shining, kilted loin-cloths, trimmed with gold leaves. The crowd drew in its breath.

"They're very young. They're just children," were the words on every lip.

The doors closed behind them. "Now!" Pablos gave Zirza a gentle push. Together they ran towards the centre of the arena, doing handsprings, turning cartwheels and somersaulting till they arrived beside Niro. Then Pablos jumped towards the bull, snapped his fingers in the bull's face and ran away. This was the signal for Niro to chase after him. Away went Pablos with the bull at his heels, head lowered, only a pace or two behind. The spectators shrieked, partly from fear for Pablos, partly from mounting excitement. Pablos quickened his pace and outstripped the bull by a short distance, turned like lightning, gripped the bull's horns and swung himself easily on to Niro's back, facing the tail. Then he swung on his hands, turned about and faced the bull's head. All this time Niro cantered the arena. The audience clapped and shouted. Pablos took a back somersault over the bull's rump and Zirza was there to steady him with her hands. Pablos touched her lightly. "You now!" he breathed in her ear. "Nothing to fear."

Zirza began to dance in front of the bull, tripping lightly as a faun. She forgot the crowd; she forgot everything save for Pablos and the bull. All at once she stood stock-still and Niro rushed towards her. The crowd held its breath. Then, light as thistledown, she gripped the horns and swung herself into a standing position on the broad back of the bull. There she pirouetted, first on one foot and then on the other while Niro ambled across the arena towards Pablos. He put his head down as though about to charge, but this was an act Pablos had rehearsed many times with him. Pablos ran forward, gripped the horns and in a second he was up beside Zirza. They looked elegant and graceful in their white, silky acrobat's uniforms, like two large white butterflies on Niro's black back. Then, together they did a double somersault over Niro's swishing tail. The applause was deafening.

"They're wonderful!" Kalamon exclaimed. "The girl is lovely."

"Yes, isn't she?" Khani agreed.

"You must be proud of them, Khani. Would you feel like selling them to me, or to the King?"

"It's a great honour you do me, Kalamon," Khani said slowly, "But they are almost like my own children. We have no children, but if we had, I should be proud if they were as fearless as those two young people."

"They are but slaves!" Amaltha said curtly, unable to control her jealousy.

"All the same, I have no wish to sell them," Khani said firmly.

A messenger touched Khani lightly on the shoulder. "The King wishes to speak with you."

Khani hastened to the King. While he was gone, Amaltha chatted with Kalamon. "It is kind of you to praise our *slaves*," she said. "I know Khani values them very much but perhaps he gives them too much credit for fearlessness."

"What makes you think that?" Kalamon asked sharply.

"They will only perform with one bull, the black one. They wouldn't do as well with another bull. In any case Khani would never permit it."

"You think that?"

"Yes, he'd refuse to allow them to do the Bull Dance with any other bull. Of course, you could ask him. For *you* he might agree, Lord Kalamon."

Just then Khani returned to his seat. He carried two beautiful gold bracelets set with precious stones.

"See!" he exclaimed proudly. "The King himself has given me these for Pablos and Zirza to mark his pleasure at their performance."

Amaltha's temper rose. *She* had not got such a beautiful bracelet among her jewels and now her slave, Zirza, was to own one. "My lord Kalamon has a question to ask you, Khani." She could not control her spiteful tone and Khani looked at her in surprise but he turned courteously to Kalamon.

"Yes, my lord?"

Kalamon looked a little put out but he had to answer.

"Your two acrobats . . . do you think they could perform equally well with another bull?"

"Perhaps. I don't know. Most acrobats leap on their own bulls," Khani answered with caution.

"Listen! If your acrobats can stand up to my best bull in the arena, it shall be yours."

"That's the fiery bull that killed an acrobat this afternoon?"

"Yes, the good bull that the crowd applauded. He's worth a lot in wagers to me."

"That would be a very severe test. My acrobats are still very young. I don't wish to try them too severely. I would rather you didn't ask that," Khani spoke respectfully but firmly.

"Not even for one leap at the bull?"

"I've given my word to Pablos that his sister shall not be tried with any bull other than the black one."

"Your word? To a *slave*? What does that count?" Amaltha said waspishly.

"My word is my honour, even to a slave. I stand by it," Khani declared. "Zirza shall not enter the arena against a strange bull."

Kalamon seized on his words. "Ah, yes, the *girl*. But you have not promised the *boy* that he shall face none but the black bull?"

"No, but they are a team."

"Come, Khani, surely the boy could stand up to a

strange bull? He has courage and confidence. If you were to put it to him that it might help you to stand well in the King's eyes . . ."

Khani knew that Kalamon was a powerful man who had the King's favour. Soon the question of a new Ruler of the King's ships would be coming up, and Khani coveted that post. He hesitated.

"I might *ask* Pablos," he said slowly. "But if he refuses that must be the end of the matter. I wouldn't force him to tackle that fierce bull against his will."

"Go, then, and ask him now, before the Bull Dancing is ended. You'll be taking the King's bracelets to him in any case."

Khani rose slowly from his seat and picked his way among the people to the aisle that gave access to the stairs. He looked saddened.

Pablos and Zirza were overjoyed at their gifts from the King. Zirza snapped the bracelet on her arm and twisted it about so that the gems sparkled in the sunlight.

"Will you give the King our humble thanks, my lord?" Pablos asked. "If there is any way we can serve him or you . . ."

"Pablos, I have been challenged by the King's Treasurer, Kalamon, to match you against a bull other than Niro."

Pablos stood very still, keeping his face a mask to hide his feelings.

"Kalamon hints that you cannot tackle any other bull," Khani began to explain unhappily.

"Master, you gave me your word that Zirza should not have to face any other bull," Pablos reminded him.

"I did not name Zirza, Pablos. I shall keep my word to you about that. It is *you* I mean. Could *you* face another bull for me? You alone? Kalamon is very powerful and he has the King's ear. If you could leap another bull, just one leap, then no more would be asked and I should stand well in Kalamon's eyes and you would have even greater honour from the crowd."

Pablos hesitated. The reply was choked in his throat. He loved Khani, and yet . . .

"If you refuse I shan't press you to do it. You're more to me than just my slave." Khani was about to turn away when Pablos laid a hand on his arm.

"Khani, master, I will do this for you. I'm not afraid, only for Zirza, so I alone must be matched against the bull. You promise that?"

"I have already promised it. I'll keep my word."

"Then I'm ready for the bull."

"No, no!" Zirza cried, clutching at his arm. "You mustn't do it, Pablos!"

"Don't be afraid, Zirza. It's for *our* honour as well as Khani's. If I tackle no bull except our own black one the crowd will soon tire of us. They'll say Niro is too tame. Sooner or later they'll shout for us to stand up to another bull. Let me do it now while I have the goodwill of the crowd to help me. Tell them to bring out Kalamon's bull, please, master."

The bull, in no good temper at being brought out again from his feed, was prodded into the ring.

"Oh!" Zirza cried, burying her face in her hands, "It is the bull that has killed an acrobat already today!"

"Ssh! Don't upset Pablos. He'll need all his confidence." Khani slipped an arm round the girl. "See! I'll stay with you here at the gate. We'll be the first to greet him when he comes out of the ring with honour," he said to comfort her. He himself was more doubtful of the outcome. At that moment he felt he could hate Kalamon.

93

Pablos had followed the bull into the ring. A loud cheer broke from the spectators when they saw the boy fearlessly facing the bull. Twenty paces separated them. The boy and the bull stared at each other. Pace by pace, slowly, never taking his eyes off the bull's eyes, Pablos advanced. Then, to everyone's surprise, the bull began to back away. A roar of laughter rose from the people at the bull's discomfiture. Suddenly the bull turned his back on Pablos and galloped away in the opposite direction. The crowd shouted their derision, but Pablos, quick as lightning, swung round and ran to face the bull as he came round the circle of the arena. The bull, taken by surprise, began to charge at him. Pablos stood his ground, his hands outstretched, ready. Then, just as the bull began to lower his head to gore the boy with his horns, Pablos made a leap for him, grasped the cruel horns, and with a bound was on his back, facing his head.

The bull was bewildered and tried to shake Pablos off but Pablos grasped his horns and hung on. "Now we'll see who's master!" he shouted at the bull.

Zirza watched fascinated as Pablos rode the bull. The bull, sweating with terror, dashed round the arena. Even Khani clapped his hands.

"Bravo, Pablos! You have done all you need. Finish now!" he shouted as Pablos and the bull careered past them. Pablos did not heed him. Once and for all he would show the crowd that he was master of the strange bull. He let go the horns and rose to his feet, poised on the bull's back, as he went again round the arena. Kalamon's men stood with a net, ready to fling it over the bull when Pablos somersaulted off his back. But just as Pablos came level with the gate disaster struck. The bull caught his foot in a rut and staggered almost to his knees. The sudden movement threw Pablos off balance and he catapulted over the bull's head. The bull was upright again quickly but Pablos had fallen on his head and was slightly dazed. His head spinning, he took longer than usual to get to his feet and staggered uncertainly. The bull regarded him angrily for a moment, his tail swishing from side to side. It was as though the animal realised that for a moment Pablos was defenceless. Now was the time for him to charge!

In that instant Zirza had slipped from Khani's grasp and pushed her way through the gate. She ran behind the bull and seized that long swinging tail and pulled her hardest! The bull gave a bellow of surprise and pain and tried to turn round to face his new aggressor, but Zirza hung on to his tail and swung with him. That instant gave Pablos time to get to his feet and steady himself. With clenched teeth he waited for the bull to swing round towards him, then, with a tremendous leap he took hold of the horns and swung on to the bull's back again, facing the tail. He held out a hand to Zirza. "Jump up! You are safer here!"

Zirza did not hesitate, but made a leap and grasped Pablos's hand. In an instant she was beside him, riding the bull. The cheers from the spectators rent the air. The bull was dazed, unable to understand his double burden. Shocked and sweating he came round to a halt beside the gate.

"Off now, quick!" Pablos cried as he saw the men with the net. Zirza slipped to the ground but she did not rush through the gate. Instead she stood in the acrobat's position to catch Pablos as he turned a somersault off the bull. In that instant Kalamon's men rushed out, armed with daggers, and flung the net over the bull's head and horns. All the fight went out of him and he ambled meekly through the gate, secured by his keepers.

It was only then that Zirza realised how great their danger had been. "Oh, Pablos! Oh, Pablos!" was all she could say amid tears.

Pablos's first reaction was anger. "Don't you ever take such a risk again!" he cried, shaken. "You might have been killed."

Zirza gave way to her storm of tears. In a moment his arms closed round her. "Don't you know how precious you are to me? I couldn't bear it if anything happened to you."

Zirza lifted her head in wonderment and strange comfort. Then, overcome by a sudden shyness she turned her tears to laughter and exclaimed, "Why, Pablos, surely I do not mean as much to you as Niro?"

Pablos began to laugh too. "Well, time will show," he said.

Khani was beside them, his eyes warm with relief. "That must be the last time. In future you'll ride only your own black bull. That is my promise to you both."

A slave came running towards them. He wore the dark-blue apron of the King's bodyguard. "The King commands you to come before him and to bring your young acrobats with you."

Zirza snatched a linen towel from a servant of the arena and hastily wiped her hands and face upon it, rearranged her tunic and drew a short cloak around her. Pablos made sure that Niro was safely haltered in his narrow byre and Khani ordered another slave to watch over the black bull.

They made their way to the King's dais. The King was seated on a wooden throne. He wore a purple mantle of Tyrian dye over his loin-tunic and jewelled belt. A plain gold circlet set with peacock's plumes confined his long flowing hair. Khani bowed very low and Pablos and Zirza knelt before him and touched their foreheads to the ground as Khani had instructed them.

"Rise, children! Come nearer and let me have a look at you," the King said gently.

In great awe of him Pablos and Zirza advanced to his feet.

"You have done very well and given us a fine performance. You are a brave girl, too," the King told Zirza as he put one finger under her chin and tilted her face up. From her seat Amaltha watched with bitter jealousy.

"Now that girl has found favour with the King too!" she thought.

"If I were to ask you what you would like for a reward, what would you choose?" the King asked.

Zirza was too shy and overwhelmed to reply but Pablos spoke for both of them.

"Your Majesty has a beautiful Palace. To us, from a far land, it seems like the home of the gods. We would beg your permission to wander round it and explore the sacred halls and the workshops and to look into the storehouses. We promise to take nothing away but just to *look*."

Zirza found her voice and added shyly, "I would like to watch the potter at work on your beautiful vases."

The King looked pleased. He loved to hear Knossos praised for it was indeed a palace above all other palaces. Even Egypt had nothing like it. "Very well! You have my permission to wander where you will, provided you first ask leave of the guardians of any chamber. I will have word sent to them and my servants shall be told not to stop you." The King turned to Khani. "And have you no reward that you would ask for yourself, Khani?"

"Only to serve Your Majesty," Khani replied with great tact.

This answer pleased the King too. "That is easily granted," he replied. "Already I have a task in my mind for you. I hear that there is unrest among my ships stationed at Thera. News has come that a soothsayer there is prophesying the destruction of my ships and sailors. It may be the usual nonsense of soothsayers, or it may be a hint of some plot against me and my ships. Whatever it is, I want you to sail at dawn and restore order. Do that well and there will be an even better post for you on your return."

Khani guessed that the King was hinting at the appointment of Ruler of his ships. He bowed very low. "I am at Your Majesty's command. I shall be ready to sail at dawn."

"Return in five days' time and report to me," the King told him. "Your wife and your slaves may continue to stay as our guests till your return and your acrobats can continue to show their skill on the black bull."

"I am grateful to Your Majesty," Khani bowed low.

The King gave a sign of dismissal and the three of them left his presence, Pablos and Zirza to return to the bull-leapers' quarters. Khani rejoined Amaltha beside Kalamon.

"Your acrobats did well. My bull is now yours," Kalamon told him.

"Thank you, my lord, that is generous of you, but with your leave I'll give him back to you. Our black bull is enough for me," Khani told him politely, but his voice was cold. "Come, Amaltha, I think we've seen enough sport with the bulls for one day. Besides, I have to make ready to go to Thera at dawn tomorrow. It's the King's command. You are to stay here till my return in five days' time."

"And what about your bull-leaping slaves?" Amaltha asked quickly.

"They are to stay here too, but they will do the Bull Dance only with their own black bull. Remember that! And now I'll escort you to the Guest House."

Khani gave his hand to raise her from her seat but Amaltha pretended not to notice it and took the hand which Kalamon offered instead. Below them the crowds were still appaluding Zirza and Pablos as they returned to the acrobats' seats. Hatred grew in Amaltha's jealous heart.

8 Earthquake!

By custom the next day was a rest day for those who had taken part in the previous day's sport. After Pablos had watered, fed and exercised Niro, he and Zirza wandered about the Palace, astonished at its wonders. The King had been as good as his word and everywhere the workmen and servants greeted them warmly, for they were the heroes of the Bull Sports.

In the long narrow store-rooms they looked in at the great 'pithoi', the storage jars that were bigger and wider than a very tall man and which lined each side of the room.

"These pithoi are for storing the olive oil," the store-keeper explained. "Our island has many olive trees so the King trades olive oil to Egypt and other countries. It's a rich trade and brings him great wealth."

"What do the King's ships bring back?" Pablos asked, interested.

"From Egypt gold, silver and ivory. From Phoenicia they come laden with tin and copper to make our bronze swords and axes. Your master, Khani, is much concerned with the King's trade. He has charge of the trade in double-axes and lamps sacred to the worship of Dhia, the Earth Mother."

"I've seen his store-rooms at Nirou Khani," Pablos told him. "Khani has ships at the little harbour there."

"They say Khani stands well in the King's favour and that soon he may be made Ruler of the King's ships. You're lucky to be the slaves of such a great man."

They wandered among pillared halls where the frescoes of the bull-leaping delighted Pablos, but Zirza liked best the frescoes of flowers and trees, birds and fishes. A fresco of leaping dolphins especially delighted her.

They climbed up the wide staircase with its dark red pillars and peered up through the vast openings that gave light to the rooms below. The King's chief steward even let them peep into the ante-chamber to the throne-room. "There's the great basin where those who come to speak with the King have to wash before they approach his presence. If you peep through that door you will see the throne."

Pablos and Zirza gasped in awe. The room glowed with colour from the frescoes that ran round three sides of it, paintings of lilies and strange mythical beasts with heads like birds and with curled manes. Stone benches lined the walls, but there was a break between them on the north wall. There stood the King's throne on a low stone plat-form. It was a simple carved chair of stone with a high back of wave-like curves, built into the wall itself. This was the throne of the most powerful Sea-King.

Pablos and Zirza crossed the great central court where noblemen and their wives gossiped under the colonnades. They visited the craftsmen's workshops on the eastern side. These were like shops with people bargaining for goods. Zirza watched the potter at his wheel with keen interest.

"I wish I could make such lovely vases!" she said to Pablos as she looked at the shelves stacked with pottery bearing designs of sea-shells, octopuses and birds in light colours on a darker clay background. The potter caught what she said and looked up.

"Why, if it isn't our little lady of the bull-leaping!

Surely you don't want to be a potter when you can leap bulls?"

"I'd much rather learn to make beautiful things," she said, pointing to the vases.

"Come and sit here, then, and I'll show you how to turn a lump of clay into a vase." He spun the wheel and turned the clay with his hand, putting his fingers at the top to hollow it inside. Before Zirza's eyes a narrow bowl emerged. The potter gathered the sides upwards in his hands to form a long neck which he hollowed out again with a finger and he created a spout at the end of it. Zirza watched fascinated as he took a pointed bone tool and traced a design of triangles and spirals on the surface of the pot and filled the outlines delicately with white paint.

"Now it must go to be fired in the oven."

Through another door was a pottery kiln with a furnace glowing beneath it.

"If you come back again tomorrow you'll see your jug," the potter promised. "But before you go, here is a little present." He took a cup shaped like a water-lily from a shelf. The cup was light as a bubble. At the base of it were black outer leaves with a vein of red. The inner petals were white against a red background.

"It looks just like a real water-lily!" Pablos cried.

"I shall treasure it always," Zirza told the potter with delight. As they left the workshop she said to Pablos, "Some day I'm going to learn to make cups and vases like that. I would rather do that than be praised for bull-leaping."

"Some day we'll both have better things to do than bull-leaping," Pablos declared.

All day they strolled about the Palace, welcomed by the

craftsmen and work-people, and praised warmly for their skill in bull-leaping.

"Tomorrow's a holiday and we'll be watching you leap the bulls again," a jeweller told them. His words sent a strange shiver down Pablos's spine.

The sun was setting in a deep red sky as Pablos took Zirza back to the women's quarters. The sea was heaving and moaning uneasily. Elena came out to meet them.

"You're to go to my lady at once," she told Zirza.

"But the King himself gave us permission to wander about the Palace today," Zirza began.

"She knows that. But she wants to see both of you on your return."

"*Both* of us? Surely she doesn't want to see me? *I'm* not her slave!" Pablos exclaimed, surprised.

"She said *both* of you. You must go with Zirza, Pablos."

When they entered Amaltha's apartment at the Guest House she was reclining on a couch, eating grapes. She looked them up and down with an impatient expression. "I suppose it didn't occur to you that I might have need of your services while you were idling round the Palace?" she asked Zirza.

Zirza flushed, but she stood her ground and answered quietly. "It was the King himself who gave us leave to explore the Palace. I'm sorry if you needed my services, my lady."

Pablos spoke up too. "We understood that this was the day of rest and holiday for the bull-leapers."

"Bull-leapers!" Amaltha flared into a temper. "You make yourselves too important. All you can do is amble round on that tame black bull!"

"We did other things yesterday, too, my lady," Pablos reminded her with spirit, his eyes sparkling angrily.

Amaltha seized on his remark. "And you will do other things again before you can rank as bull-leapers. Tomorrow you will *both* be faced with other strange bulls, fiercer than that stupid black animal. *Then* we shall see how you will fare."

Pablos turned white. He was not afraid for himself but for Zirza. He knew they had not been matched against other bulls as most of the acrobats had. He knew, too, that the life of an acrobat was rated at not more than three or four months. He spoke quickly. "But my lord Khani would not wish it."

Amaltha grew hot with temper. "The Lord Khani is not here. When he is away *I* rule his household and his slaves. You will obey *me,*" she spat at them. "I've promised my lord Kalamon that you'll be matched against a better bull than yesterday's. You'll do as you are told, or I'll have you whipped."

"*I* will tackle any bull but the Lord Khani gave me his word that Zirza should not be faced with a strange bull," Pablos persisted.

"How dare you speak so impudently to me!" Amaltha shouted. "Take care or I'll have you flogged so you have no strength to fight against any bulls tomorrow."

Zirza implored her, "Please, please do not harm Pablos. *I* will do anything you wish . . ."

"You will do what I wish, whether you like it or not. You are *my* slave to do with as I please, to *sell* if I like . . ."

"No, no!" Pablos protested.

Amaltha turned to him with a bitter mocking smile. "Ah! That threat brings you to your senses, does it? Listen to me! Tomorrow you *both* separately tackle any bull sent against you. If you refuse to leap it or prove cowards in the ring, then I will have Zirza lashed and put in a ship by sunset and sold in an Egyptian slave-market. Then you will never see her again."

"Pablos! Pablos! I would rather risk the Bull Sports," Zirza cried.

"If only my lord Khani knew of this . . .!" Pablos said wildly.

"Another word from you and I'll have your tongue cut out!" Amaltha declared. "Tomorrow you will both show what you are made of in the Bull Sports. Go away now, both of you, before I send for slaves with whips."

They both knew that she was capable of any cruelty when she was in such a temper and they hurried away before she could carry out her threat. Zirza was sobbing with indignation and terror.

"She . . . she *hates* me! What have I done to her that she wants to see me killed?"

"Ssh! Ssh, Zirza! Surely we can do something?"

"What? What can we do? She has us both in her power," Zirza wept.

Pablos racked his brains. "If only we could gain *time* till Khani's return! Only one or two days at the most and he might be here! If only we could hide . . ."

"Amaltha would have Kalamon ransack the Palace for us," Zirza sounded despairing.

"The Palace, yes, but we won't hide in the Palace."

"Where then?"

"In the forest above Nirou Khani. There we can watch for Khani's return. Amaltha would never think to look for us near her home."

"Shall we start *now*?" Zirza asked.

"No. It's still daylight and Amaltha might send for you again before she goes to bed. We'll have to wait till she's asleep and the women too. Then you can slip out in the darkness and go round to the West Court. Hide in the shadow of the store-houses and don't move till you hear me whistle."

"All right."

"Meanwhile I'll take out Niro as though I'm going to exercise him and I'll tether him on the hill and come back to the bull-leapers' quarters by another way."

"Niro? Must Niro go too? Won't he give us away to anyone who comes looking for us?"

"Zirza, we'll have to take a chance on that. Niro brought us safely through the waves and he's brought us good fortune at Knossos. He's our friend. Don't ask me to part with him."

Zirza knew how strongly Pablos felt about the black bull. She gave a sigh but she said, "All right, I suppose he must go with us."

"Listen, Zirza! We must all stick together. We were meant for better things than making sport for the crowds."

Just then the earth trembled slightly under their feet.

"What was that?" Zirza cried, clutching his arm.

Pablos quickly recovered his composure. "It's the Sea-God trying his strength at shaking the earth." Pablos had been brought up in the old beliefs of Corinth. "There! It was nothing much. Everything's quiet again. Maron told me there are sometimes earthquakes in the island but they are nothing to fear. Go to the women's quarters at once in case Amaltha has been disturbed and sends for her slaves. Then go to bed early and rest. We've a long way to go tonight."

Zirza trusted Pablos. She promised to do as he said.

"Start out for the hiding place by the store-houses as soon as all the women are asleep."

"You'll take care, too, Pablos?" There was love and anxiety in her voice.

"I'll take care, if only for your sake."

They clasped hands for a moment and then Pablos was gone. Zirza returned to the Guest House, but not to sleep. The people in the Palace had been disturbed by the slight earth-tremor and it was some time before the women could leave Amaltha and settle in their beds. At last all was quiet and Zirza could tell by their even breathing that the women were asleep. She had not undressed but no one had remarked on this for many people had gone to sleep in their clothes after the small earth shake, in case another should occur.

Silently Zirza rose and, moving like a mouse, she reached the door. Only one person was aware of her going and that was Elena. She watched Zirza open the door into the court, a dark shadow against the stars. Then Elena rose too and wrapped a dark cloak around herself and prepared to follow Zirza.

Pablos hitched Niro to an olive tree in the groves on the southern hillside above the river gorge and then returned cautiously to the Palace. Away on the northern horizon a strange light flickered, and layers of smoky cloud were red-hued. Pablos stopped to look.

"What is happening over the sea? Surely the island of Thera lies there?" he asked himself.

At that moment the island of Thera itself seemed to explode and to rise in the air and be shattered into thousands of rocks among the clouds! Pablos opened his mouth to cry out for at first the explosion seemed without sound. But the sound-waves travelled fast, and so did the shock waves of a terrific earthquake. Just as the sound of the exploding volcano reached Crete the ground shook terribly and great rents and gulfs opened in the rocky surface.

Pablos was deafened and flung to the ground. The noise was tremendous, even though Thera was a long distance away. It was as though the whole world had split apart. The ground quivered beneath him as he struggled to his hands and knees. A terrible red light from Thera shone over the sea and lit up the scene like a nightmare below him. As he looked at it the Palace of Knossos shook and crumbled before his eyes. The two watch-towers near the northern gateway toppled and fell like a house of cards collapsing. The noise of their fall added to the uproar of the volcano on Thera. Great slabs of masonry were hurled into the air. Screams and wails rose from the ruins. Pablos rose unsteadily to his feet and stared. Beyond the Palace, at the port of Amnisos, the sea had been heaped up and plucked back as though a giant hand had gathered up the waters. The sea-bed was laid bare. Rocks rolled about in it as though stirred like porridge. Near the horizon the red light in the sky showed a huge wall of water piling up. It was advancing towards Crete at a great speed.

Pablos lurched to his feet. Zirza? Where was she? He had told her to hide under the shadow of the West Wall, the outer wall of the store-rooms, and the walls of Knossos were still tottering and falling everywhere as yet another shake of the earth toppled them. At night the Palace of Knossos was lit by hundreds of oil lamps—wicks of sheep's wool floating in open shallow bowls of olive oil. The lamps were flung about in the shaking rooms. Some fell upon curtains and rugs and wooden furnishings. The live coals in the potter's furnace were scattered widely around and the red embers from the cooking fires in the kitchens flew through the air and started a hundred other fires.

Soon the Palace was ablaze in a hundred places and the smoke and dust drifted up the hillside to Pablos.

Zirza? He *must* find Zirza. He tried to hurry down the hill towards Knossos but great yawning crevices had opened in his path and he had to pick his steps by the light from the lurid flames of Knossos and the red skies over the sea. Once he paused to get his breath and looked out towards the sea. He gave a gasp of horror. A great mountain of sea-water was nearing Crete. Toppling crests of water shone red like blood in the light of Thera's volcano. Soon the tremendous tidal wave would reach the shores of the port below Knossos. How high would it reach? Pablos began to run again. He must reach Knossos before the new doom fell. He must find Zirza, if she was still alive. His heart almost stopped beating at the thought of her under those toppled walls.

Still under his feet smaller earth tremors occurred, echoes of the first tremendous shock wave, but Pablos stumbled on. The east side of the Palace lay in ruins; the great pillars of the halls and colonnades lying across each other. Upper rooms had collapsed into those below them and the great staircase ended abruptly in mid-air, as though it had been sliced off by a huge axe. Everywhere flames arose, with thick smoke. The stench of burning was horrible. People tried to crawl out like ants from a destroyed ant-heap. They were the ones who had been lucky enough to get out of the Palace. Many lay dead and dying under the ruined walls.

Pablos pounded his way along towards the west side of the Palace where the great store-rooms were. The walls had split apart and the giant pithoi, the storage jars, were rolled on their sides, oil flowing from them and grain spilling out on the ground. Pablos felt sick at heart. Zirza could never have lived in the midst of all this destruction. "Zirza! Zirza!" he called wildly as he reached the half-fallen walls on the west side. Here the ruin was not quite so complete as on the eastern side of the Palace. Sections of wall still stood, though the store-rooms were open to the sky.

"Zirza! Zirza!" he continued to shout, but in the uproar of walls still falling and the sound of raging fires he could hear no reply. Still he shouted, "Zirza! Zirza! It's Pablos! Answer me! Answer me!"

He stopped and listened. He could hear no answering voice at all. He picked his way over the crashed pithoi, still calling desperately. Then, suddenly, by the flaring light of flames, he saw something sticking out from the neck of a huge fallen but unbroken pithoi. It was a white hand and arm and on it was the bracelet that the King had given to Zirza!

Pablos knelt beside the pithoi and tugged at the hand. It was not cold but warm with the warmth of life.

"Zirza! Come out! It's Pablos! I'm here."

The arm stirred feebly and emerged a little further.

"Zirza! Are you all right?" Pablos cried.

A weak voice answered him, muffled by the jar. "I . . . I . . . Is it you, Pablos?"

Pablos thrust his arms into the pithoi to pull her out, shielding her shoulders and hips from bruising against the sides. She crawled out towards him. In another minute she was out of the giant jar and in his arms.

"Oh, Pablos, Pablos! What happened?" she cried as she clung to him.

"A great earthquake! It came from the sea, from Thera. The Palace is in ruins and on fire. Can you stand, Zirza? We must get away from here at once."

Zirza rose unsteadily to her feet. "I . . . I crawled into the empty pithoi to protect me when the walls fell outward."

"Try to walk, Zirza! We *must* get up the hill. There's a great wave coming over the sea. Any minute now it'll strike the island and may cause another earthquake." Pablos tugged at her hand.

Fear lent Zirza the power to move her limbs again. They raced for the hill. When they were half-way up it the towering wave crashed into the island with a terrible roar.

"Down! Get down! Lie down!" Pablos pushed Zirza to the ground.

Another shock wave struck the island: more of the Palace walls crumbled but no cleft opened near Pablos and Zirza. When the earth ceased to shake and all was quiet again save for the roar of the sea and the Palace fires, Pablos ventured to raise his head. There was still the red glow over Thera that seemed to light up the world. The sea had not reached the Palace but he could see nothing of the harbour beyond, nor the houses and warehouses that surrounded it. The red glow from over the sea was becoming dimmed by a strange fog. Instinct told Pablos they must find some kind of shelter.

He pulled Zirza to her feet. "Hurry! Run! We must get up the hill. There's a small cave I know."

They reached the thicket where Pablos had tied Niro. Pablos did not wait to untie him but plucked the bronze dagger from his belt and cut the straw rope, then he urged the bull along. Niro was inclined to amble so Pablos snapped a willow switch from a tree and struck Niro smartly on the rump with it. It was the first time in his life he had ever struck the bull. Niro plunged with the shock but he quickened his pace to a trot. They reached a cleft between two high rocks.

"In there!" Pablos pointed.

Zirza hesitated. "What if there's another earthquake? We might be buried there."

"We'll have to risk that, but the cave has a good strong roof and sides. It has stood up to the big earthquake. We *must* find shelter."

"What from?"

Pablos pointed seaward where the strange dark cloud was blotting out the stars. A hot wind swept over them.

"That! I don't know what it is but I'm afraid of it. We mustn't be caught in it. We must get out of this burning wind. Follow me!" and urging the bull before him Pablos went downward into the cave.

It was cool and quiet there after the heat and turmoil outside. Somewhere quite near and just below them a stream tinkled. In the darkness Pablos did not dare to go very far. His hands encountered a limestone pillar. He knew there were pillars in the caves about Knossos. Maron had told him of them. This pillar seemed to taper upwards. Pablos hitched the remains of the straw rope about it to stop Niro from wandering and breaking a leg in some rocky cleft.

"There's a smooth rock here," he told Zirza. "We'll sit here and wait for daybreak. It shouldn't be long now."

Exhausted they sank down and fell into an uneasy sleep.

It seemed to Pablos that they had been asleep for a long time but the mouth of the cave was still dark when he awoke. There was a queer smell of brimstone in the air. Zirza stirred beside him and the bull was very restless. Pablos felt hungry. He woke Zirza. "My stomach tells me it's time to eat. I'm going to the mouth of the cave to see what's happening outside. You stay here."

It was an eerie twilight outside, scarcely any daylight filtering through a large heavy cloud that enveloped the island. It was thicker than a fog and it made Pablos cough. His feet seemed to sink in the grass of the hillside but when he looked down at them there was no grass there. Instead there was a strange reddish-grey substance. Pablos lifted some of it in his hand and it trickled through his fingers like sand. It was *ash*! Everywhere there was a deep layer of ash into which his feet sank. At first Pablos thought it had come from the burning of the Palace, then he realised that not even the Palace fires would bring such deep layers of ash up the hillside. Besides, the fine ash was still falling. Already he felt it on his skin. It must have come from that tremendous explosion over the sea on Thera, the island with the volcano that smoked by day and burned by night. This was the cloud that had blotted out the stars and filled him with dread. His instinct had been right to seek shelter from it. There was nothing to do but to go back to the cave and wait there till the ash had ceased falling. Already it was choking him. He regained the cave and thankfully plunged into its depths, coughing hard.

"What's the matter? What have you found?" Zirza cried.

"*Ash*! Ash lying thick on the ground everywhere. I ... I must get down to the water and drink. I'm choking!"

He felt his way down the easy slope to the stream. Zirza followed him.

"Look! I have a cup." She withdrew it from the folds of her cloak. "It's the one the potter gave me. Take it. The rock is too steep for you to lean over and put your mouth into the stream."

Pablos filled it and drank, then filled it again for Zirza to drink. The water was crystal clear and pure.

"At least we have good fresh water," he said. "I've heard that men can live for days on water alone. We may have to do that. I must feel my way about to try to find an easy path for Niro to get down to the water. He'll need to drink too."

"Will we . . . will we have to stay here long?" Zirza faltered.

"Till the ash has stopped falling. Who knows how long that might take?"

Zirza was determined to put a brave front on it. "There's one good thing. Amaltha won't be able to send out a search party to look for me or to make me face fierce bulls today."

"Amaltha won't be able to make you leap fierce bulls any day," Pablos told her. "Even if she's still alive there'll be no more Bull Sports for many a long day, if ever again. The Palace is in ruins and burning."

"Oh, Pablos!" Zirza was shocked by the realisation. She had seen walls toppled by the earthquake but had not realised how terrible the damage had been. "Where shall we go, then?"

"Perhaps to Nirou Khani to see what has happened there. Perhaps my lord Khani . . ." Pablos's voice faltered. Khani had put out in the King's ship to go to Thera! There was little hope that any ship could have lived in those terrible boiling mountainous seas, even if they had survived the frightful explosion of the volcano.

"We'll just have to stay here and wait for the ash to stop falling," Pablos said grimly. "Meanwhile I'll get Niro down to the water. At least we have a stream and we won't die of thirst."

Zirza felt in the pocket of her cloak. "And I have a piece of honey cake I saved for us to eat on our journey. We can divide it into three."

"Into six!" Pablos decided. "That way it'll make us a small meal for today and another for tomorrow."

9 The New Beginning

All that day the ash continued to fall, light as snow, fine and deadly. Several times Pablos ventured to the mouth of the cave, to find little change, except that towards noon the dark cloud did not seem quite so dark. Then, as the day advanced, it grew dark again.

"The ash is still falling," he told Zirza. "We'll have to stay here. There's nothing else we can do."

"What will we do for food when the honey cake's finished?"

"Just drink water, that's all we can do—and be glad this is an underground stream that the ash can't reach. The ash can't go on falling for ever."

In spite of his brave words Pablos felt that his stomach was very empty. He was troubled too about Niro. Soon the bull would need to eat and where was he to find grass?

"We may as well try to sleep," he told Zirza. "While we're sleeping we're not using up our strength."

Zirza shivered. "It's so cold in here. I'm too cold to sleep."

"Niro is warm. I'll tell him to lie down and we'll huddle up close to his back."

Niro obediently settled down on the flat rock. He seemed glad to feel Zirza and Pablos close to him. Perhaps he felt cold and frightened too. Zirza nestled up against Niro's back and Pablos put an arm around her. Soon, from the warmth of Niro and the comfort of Pablos's arm, she fell asleep. Pablos lay awake for a long time, thinking of many things, then he too slept.

116

When he awoke it was to a strange pattering sound outside the cave. The stream in the cave was running much higher too and lapping over the stones, quite near to them. It had become a rushing torrent. There was daylight at the cave mouth, a gray misty daylight with no sun, but at least it was day. Pablos got up and went to look outside. The ash was no longer falling but rain had taken its place, torrents of warm rain that raised steam from the still warm ash on the ground. Pablos rushed back to tell Zirza.

"It's raining! It's raining!" he cried with joy. "The ash fall has stopped."

Zirza started up. "Can we go out then, now?"

Pablos would have liked to rush out into the rain too but he restrained himself. "Not yet! We must wait for the rain to stop."

"First we had to wait for the ash to stop falling and now the rain!" Zirza exclaimed in exasperation.

"Listen, Zirza! Rain falling on that ash will just made a sea of mud. Our feet would sink into it. The ash will lie even deeper down the hill. We must wait till the rain stops and the sun comes out to dry up the mud."

"So now we have to wait for the sun too?"

"The sun is always hot over the island. Once it has hardened the mud, then we can venture out. Let's sit down and talk."

"What about?"

"Ourselves. What we're going to do when we leave here."

"*If* we leave here . . ." Zirza cried despairingly.

"Don't be afraid. We *will* leave here."

"Where shall we go? If the Palace is destroyed . . ."

"There would be no life for us in the Palace any more.

The bull-leaping is over. No one will want acrobats, but people will still need bulls. And we have a bull, a good bull."

"You're always thinking of the bull," Zirza said a little sadly, "but what's the good of a bull if the Bull Sports are finished?"

"Bulls are not created just for sport." Pablos spoke seriously. "They were first meant to father herds of cattle. People need cattle for meat and milk and to help to plough the ground. They will need good bulls to breed new herds of cattle. After this earthquake there will be a shortage of good bulls in Crete and Niro is a good bull. We must become cattle farmers. After all, when I was in Corinth I was slave to a cattle farmer, so that's something I know about."

"But it'll take time to breed a herd of cattle and we'll need cows too," Zirza said practically. She had been brought up in a nomad tribe whose wealth was in their cattle.

"You're right but Maron told me of farms in the valleys over the mountains. The earthquake may not have reached them. But first I want to go and see what has happened at Knossos."

"But Amaltha might be there. She'd make slaves of us again." Zirza did not want Amaltha to find her.

"I don't think we'll ever be slaves again but I must go to the Palace and find out what's happened to the people we knew. But while we wait we can sit at the entrance to the cave and watch for the rain to stop."

The torrential rain was washing long rivulets of mud down the hill. The bed of the Karaitos River was brimming over. When the rain slackened a little they were able to see the Palace. The whole of the eastern side was in

"Oh, Pablos!" Zirza was stunned by the horror of it all. "If you hadn't found me I would have been among them. I . . . I . . ." Then a sudden thought struck her. "Elena? Was Elena one of them?"

"I didn't see her but I'll go back and make sure."

When he returned he told Zirza, "She isn't there."

"Where can she be, then?" Zirza cried wildly.

Pablos shook his head. He knew there was little hope. "She might have been in the women's quarters behind the King's apartments. The . . . the whole place is buried beneath the fallen walls. No one could have lived. It . . . death . . . would be quick."

Zirza began to sob. "Elena! Elena was kind to me . . ."

"There's nothing we can do," Pablos told her. "We'll work our way round to the store-rooms and see if we can find food for ourselves and Niro."

He guided the bull round the fallen boulders to the West Court. The strong west wall of the store-rooms was still standing but there were many gaps in it and Pablos could see into the store-rooms. Though most of the pithoi were fallen and broken, some were still whole.

"Hold the bull while I take a look," Pablos said.

He climbed through a gap and found he was in a grain store. Some pithoi lay on their sides, unbroken, and from the necks of the huge jars a stream of wheat grains had fallen out. Here, at least was food for Niro, but for themselves it would have to be ground into flour. He looked around him. Through an open gap to the next room he spied a grindstone. Near it was the saddle-stone which the millers had used for grinding the wheat to flour on the grindstone. They would be too heavy to carry. Pablos decided they would have to find suitable stones for grinding as they made their journey over the mountains. First, though, he would carry some of the grain to Niro. On the strength of the bull depended their escape to a part of the island not entirely devastated by the earthquake. He hunted about again for something in which to carry the grain. From a stone hook in the half-fallen wall hung a large sheepskin pouch, the kind he had carried as a herd-boy. He was beginning to fill it with handfuls of grain when he heard a faint noise, more a moan than a cry. It came from the next room.

Pablos clambered over the rubble and into the passage beyond and with difficulty he made his way into the narrow store-room.

"Is anyone there?" he shouted. He was answered by another faint cry that came from a narrow doorway in a connecting wall. The door had fallen and on top of it lay the lintel beam and some large wall stones. Pablos peered under the door. Someone was crouched there, wedged in a gap made by the door on top of the fallen masonry. It was impossible for anyone imprisoned beneath the door to move it, for it was wedged tight by the lintel beam.

"Hold on! Keep still! I'll get you out," Pablos said. "But I'll need to try and get help."

A feeble voice answered him. "Help me! Be quick!"

Pablos climbed out on to the West Court where Zirza was holding the bull. "Dare you come with me? There's someone alive imprisoned under a door and fallen stones. I need help to lift the door."

Zirza did not hesitate. "I'll come," she said at once.

Pablos hitched Niro's rope to a boulder and he and Zirza climbed back along the narrow passage into the store-room. They moved the rubble off the door and together they managed to lift the beam that wedged it but cave he said, "You climb on to Niro's back, Zirza. We'l go quicker that way. You only have thin sandals and the ash would cut your feet. I have leather boots."

The three of them made their way slowly down the hill.

"Our best hope is on the west side of the Palace where the earthquake doesn't seem to have done as much damage," Pablos decided.

Everywhere was horrible destruction. Stone pillars and wooden beams had collapsed. Where once the towers stood were huge heaps of rubble. A pall of the reddish-grey ash lay over everything. From the smouldering ruins came a stench of fire and death. Near the doors lay the bodies of those inhabitants who had rushed to escape and been caught by the falling walls and suffocated by the smoke from the fires and the rain of ash. Here and there one or two people were scrabbling among the debris looking for loved ones or lost treasures. Zirza shuddered and even Pablos felt sick but he urged the bull on past the terrible sights, past the south corridor and round the angle of the building to the west. They arrived at the Guest House, or what remained of it.

"Wait here with the bull," Pablos ordered Zirza. "I'll try to take a look inside."

Zirza knew why and shivered with fear. In a few minutes Pablos was back, his face white and shocked.

"You'll never be a slave to Amaltha again. She was there by the door, pinned down by a beam. She . . . she's quite dead," he stammered.

"The other slaves? The women? Where are they?" Zirza gasped.

"They were lying about her, dead too. The ones who hadn't been struck by falling beams and stones had been suffocated by the smoke and ash."

ruins and all the great towers were gone. Zirza clapped her hands in horror.

"All the places where people worked, the jewellers' shops, the potter's workshop, they're just heaps of stone!"

Pablos was staring out to the sea beyond Knossos. "The harbour of Amnisos!" he exclaimed. "Where are the harbour walls and the long piers? And the ships? Where are the warehouses and the noblemen's houses? The sea has covered them all!"

There was no trace of the proud ships that had once brought trade to Amnisos, only a heaving mass of angry grey waters. Pablos's hopes of Khani's safety faded at once. No ship could survive in such a sea. He looked anxiously down the hillside. Soon he would have to find food for them both and for the bull too. There would be no grass fit to eat under that covering of ash. His only hope was that he might find fodder at Knossos that had not been destroyed in the fire, enough to feed the bull till they might reach pasture on the other side of the island.

The rain ceased and the clouds rolled away to reveal a hot sun. Soon its rays gained in power and steam rose from the mud. Within a couple of hours the mud was beginning to dry and crack and harden. Pablos ventured outside the cave and found that on the western side of the hill the ash had not fallen so thickly as just below the cave. Their feet might not sink so deeply in it, especially the bull's. He went back to the cave.

"We'll try to get down to Knossos to find food," he told Zirza.

Though she shivered at the idea of going back to the Palace and perhaps encountering Amaltha, Zirza knew they could not go much longer without food. Pablos unhitched Niro from the pillar and at the mouth of the hough, he would carry some of the grain to Niro. On he strength of the bull depended their escape to a part of he island not entirely devastated by the earthquake. He hunted about again for something in which to carry the grain. From a stone hook in the half-fallen wall hung a large sheepskin pouch, the kind he had carried as a herd-boy. He was beginning to fill it with handfuls of grain when he heard a faint noise, more a moan than a cry. It came from the next room.

Pablos clambered over the rubble and into the passage beyond and with difficulty he made his way into the narrow store-room.

"Is anyone there?" he shouted. He was answered by another faint cry that came from a narrow doorway in a connecting wall. The door had fallen and on top of it lay the lintel beam and some large wall stones. Pablos peered under the door. Someone was crouched there, wedged in a gap made by the door on top of the fallen masonry. It was impossible for anyone imprisoned beneath the door to move it, for it was wedged tight by the lintel beam.

"Hold on! Keep still! I'll get you out," Pablos said. "But I'll need to try and get help."

A feeble voice answered him. "Help me! Be quick!"

Pablos climbed out on to the West Court where Zirza was holding the bull. "Dare you come with me? There's someone alive imprisoned under a door and fallen stones. I need help to lift the door."

Zirza did not hesitate. "I'll come," she said at once.

Pablos hitched Niro's rope to a boulder and he and Zirza climbed back along the narrow passage into the store-room. They moved the rubble off the door and together they managed to lift the beam that wedged it but

ruins and all the great towers were gone. Zirza clapped her hands in horror.

"All the places where people worked, the jewellers' shops, the potter's workshop, they're just heaps of stone!"

Pablos was staring out to the sea beyond Knossos. "The harbour of Amnisos!" he exclaimed. "Where are the harbour walls and the long piers? And the ships? Where are the warehouses and the noblemen's houses? The sea has covered them all!"

There was no trace of the proud ships that had once brought trade to Amnisos, only a heaving mass of angry grey waters. Pablos's hopes of Khani's safety faded at once. No ship could survive in such a sea. He looked anxiously down the hillside. Soon he would have to find food for them both and for the bull too. There would be no grass fit to eat under that covering of ash. His only hope was that he might find fodder at Knossos that had not been destroyed in the fire, enough to feed the bull till they might reach pasture on the other side of the island.

The rain ceased and the clouds rolled away to reveal a hot sun. Soon its rays gained in power and steam rose from the mud. Within a couple of hours the mud was beginning to dry and crack and harden. Pablos ventured outside the cave and found that on the western side of the hill the ash had not fallen so thickly as just below the cave. Their feet might not sink so deeply in it, especially the bull's. He went back to the cave.

"We'll try to get down to Knossos to find food," he told Zirza.

Though she shivered at the idea of going back to the Palace and perhaps encountering Amaltha, Zirza knew they could not go much longer without food. Pablos unhitched Niro from the pillar and at the mouth of the

cave he said, "You climb on to Niro's back, Zirza. We'l
go quicker that way. You only have thin sandals and the
ash would cut your feet. I have leather boots."

The three of them made their way slowly down the hill.

"Our best hope is on the west side of the Palace where
the earthquake doesn't seem to have done as much
damage," Pablos decided.

Everywhere was horrible destruction. Stone pillars and
wooden beams had collapsed. Where once the towers
stood were huge heaps of rubble. A pall of the reddish-
grey ash lay over everything. From the smouldering ruins
came a stench of fire and death. Near the doors lay the
bodies of those inhabitants who had rushed to escape and
been caught by the falling walls and suffocated by the
smoke from the fires and the rain of ash. Here and there
one or two people were scrabbling among the debris
looking for loved ones or lost treasures. Zirza shuddered
and even Pablos felt sick but he urged the bull on past the
terrible sights, past the south corridor and round the angle
of the building to the west. They arrived at the Guest
House, or what remained of it.

"Wait here with the bull," Pablos ordered Zirza. "I'll
try to take a look inside."

Zirza knew why and shivered with fear. In a few
minutes Pablos was back, his face white and shocked.

"You'll never be a slave to Amaltha again. She was
there by the door, pinned down by a beam. She . . . she's
quite dead," he stammered.

"The other slaves? The women? Where are they?"
Zirza gasped.

"They were lying about her, dead too. The ones who
hadn't been struck by falling beams and stones had been
suffocated by the smoke and ash."

"Oh, Pablos!" Zirza was stunned by the horror o
"If you hadn't found me I would have been among
I . . . I . . ." Then a sudden thought struck her. "Elen
Elena one of them?"

"I didn't see her but I'll go back and make sure
When he returned he told Zirza, "She isn't ther

"Where can she be, then?" Zirza cried wildly.

Pablos shook his head. He knew there was litt
"She might have been in the women's quarters bel
King's apartments. The . . . the whole place is
beneath the fallen walls. No one could have lived
death . . . would be quick."

Zirza began to sob. "Elena! Elena was kind to

"There's nothing we can do," Pablos told her
work our way round to the store-rooms and see i
find food for ourselves and Niro."

He guided the bull round the fallen boulder
West Court. The strong west wall of the store-ro
still standing but there were many gaps in it an
could see into the store-rooms. Though most of t
were fallen and broken, some were still whole.

"Hold the bull while I take a look," Pablos sa

He climbed through a gap and found he was
store. Some pithoi lay on their sides, unbroken,
the necks of the huge jars a stream of wheat g
fallen out. Here, at least was food for Niro, but
selves it would have to be ground into flour. H
around him. Through an open gap to the next
spied a grindstone. Near it was the saddle-stone
millers had used for grinding the wheat to flo
grindstone. They would be too heavy to car
decided they would have to find suitable stones
ing as they made their journey over the mount

the door was of thick wood and almost too heavy for them.

"We can't lift it. We must try sliding it sideways," Pablos decided. There was a danger that if the heavy door hit a wall it would bring the tottering masonry down on them.

"Stand clear over there, Zirza. The wall may collapse." For once Zirza defied him. "No! It will take both of us to move the door. If you're buried under a wall I would rather die with you," she declared.

They both pushed hard at the door and at last the stone that was holding it moved enough for them to shift the door to open a gap. Beneath it the figure of a woman stirred feebly and her hands came up to grasp the ones outstretched to her. With a tremendous effort they hauled her out of the hole.

Zirza gave a cry. "It's Elena! Elena, Elena! We thought you'd died under the ruins in the Guest House."

Elena was gasping, her lips cracked and blackened. "Water! Water!" she moaned.

"Where will we get water?" Zirza cried desperately.

Pablos was at a loss too. There was a well across the West Court but he had seen already that it was choked with rubble and the leather bucket had disappeared. Then he remembered the wine jars in the end store.

"Give me your cup. I'll find some wine," he told Zirza.

He was lucky. Though most of the wine jars had been shattered in the earthquake, three remained standing in a corner and they contained sweet wine. He returned with the cup brimming over and held it to Elena's lips. She drank thirstily and began to revive. Pablos fetched another cup of wine. Zirza felt Elena's hands and feet and rubbed them and felt her limbs for any broken bones. Elena's arms and legs, though bruised, were unbroken. She came to her senses and stared at Zirza.

"Zirza, child! I thought you had been killed."

"And we thought you'd died with Amaltha and the other women slaves!" Zirza exclaimed.

Pablos told her of the fate of those in the Guest House and tears came into Elena's eyes at the thought of her fellow slaves.

"If it hadn't been for you, Zirza, I should have been with them and died too. I saw you creep from your bed and out of the door and I followed you to make sure you would come to no harm. When you hid in the corner of the wall I guessed Pablos would be coming for you, so I crept inside a store-room to wait and see if I was right. It was then that the earthquake came and the walls fell around me. When I came to my senses I was trapped and the black dark was over me. What happened to the Palace?"

Zirza told her of the destruction of Knossos.

"And the King? And his people? What about the people?"

"There is no sign of the King but his part of the Palace is a ruin. Many people have died and those who escaped death must have fled from the ruins for fear of more earthquakes," Pablos told her. "Soon they'll be coming back, though, to see what's left and some men will come to loot what treasures they can find. They mustn't find my black bull. Try to stand, please, Elena, so we can get away from here before the looters come."

Elena made a great effort and she and Zirza made their way over the rubble to the gap that gave on to the West Court. Pablos turned back into the store-rooms to look for other food that would sustain them on the journey they must take. When he rejoined Zirza and Elena he was carrying a linen sack and a narrow-necked vase.

"What have you got there?" Zirza asked.

He handed the vase to her. "Something that you and Elena used to put into those large flat cakes, *honey*!" He shook the sack. "And here are carob beans. These will feed us and the bull till we reach a place that the earthquake hasn't touched. With carob beans and honey and corn for Niro we'll have strength enough for our journey."

"But where are we going?" Zirza asked.

"Maron once told me that beyond the mountains to the south there is a plain, the Plain of Messara, crossed by two rivers with many smaller rivers running into them. The King's father had another palace there, the Palace of Phaistos that Maron knew when he was a boy."

"But if we go to another palace we'll only be made into slaves again," Zirza said unhappily.

"We won't go to the Palace. We'll stop where we come down from the mountains to the plain. There by the river, Maron told me his brother had a farm. He might be glad of help in his fields. How I wish Maron had lived, though, to come with us and show us the way. He was kind to me and we talked a lot together."

"But Maron is *not* lying under the ruins of Knossos!" Elena cried. "Only the day before the earthquake he was sent by Khani to arrange for cattle to be sent to Nirou Khani."

"Then he'll be at the farm?" Pablos said with joy.

"If he hasn't gone to Nirou Khani."

"Will we be going to Nirou Khani?" Zirza asked.

Pablos shook his head. "There'll be little of Nirou Khani left. It stands nearer to the sea than Knossos. It can't have escaped the earthquake. No, we'll make for the

Plain of Messara. We must be on our way before sunset."

"But where shall we rest at night?" Zirza asked.

"Maron said there were many caves in the mountains along the way. With caves for shelter and the river for water and the food we carry we'll do well enough. But we must reach fresh springs before nightfall."

Zirza looked back a little sadly at the ruins of Knossos.

"We'll never do the bull-leaping there again with the people clapping their hands and shouting our names and the King sending gifts to us," she said as she fingered the bracelet on her arm. There was regret in her voice for the moments of glory they had known.

"It wouldn't have lasted, Zirza," Pablos said. "The life of any bull-leaper, however quick, was only reckoned a few months. Sooner or later we'd have been gored by a bull and the crowds would soon have forgotten us and cheered fresh favourites. It would have been short-lived glory. What we shall do now will last us all our lives and bring us and others peace and happiness."

"You're right. That's what I feel too, but what are we going to do now?" Zirza looked trustingly at Pablos.

"We'll till the land and grow grain for our own bread: we'll grow fruit and make wine and get oil from our own olive trees." Pablos spoke with growing confidence, his eyes looking into the future. "We'll raise a herd of cattle with Niro as their sire. And we . . ." He hesitated only for a minute. "We'll find Maron and for a time we'll be his children. Soon we'll be of an age to marry and we shall build a house for ourselves, and you will no longer be my sister but my wife."

"That is well spoken," Elena said gently, and Zirza looked at him with shining eyes and held out her hands to him.